TRAIL OF SECRETS

WAGON TRAIN MATCHES
BOOK 2

LACY WILLIAMS

ONE

Stella Fairfax wouldn't call herself an expert at hiding in plain sight, but she'd done it for long enough that it had become second nature.

Wrap her chest beneath a man's shirt.

Keep her hat low on her head.

Walk with a swagger she never truly felt.

She was Stephen, as far as anyone on this wagon train to Oregon was concerned.

"How much longer do we have to do this?" Her sister Lily, younger by almost four years, asked the question like a complaint as she sat on the bench seat of their family wagon.

Lily was in disguise, too. She was dressed as Louis Fairfax, though she wasn't as practiced at the disguise as Stella. She sat slouched in the wagon seat with the reins dangling from her hands and her hat pulled low over her face.

Next to her, Stella rode the massive black stallion beside the wagon.

Dusk was gathering around them and Stella couldn't

help wondering why the wagon master, Hollis Tremblay, hadn't yet called a halt for the day.

Stephen wasn't a very good horseman. Mostly because Stella hadn't actually been astride a horse in all of her twenty-three years. Not until they'd reached Independence, Missouri, just before they'd set out on this long journey across the country.

The horse had known she wasn't a strong rider from the very beginning. He'd unseated her before they'd rolled out from Independence. And again four days ago, even though she'd become a master at clinging to his saddle.

Today, he seemed extra ornery, his power barely harnessed by the reins she held in her left hand.

Her right forearm still ached from how she'd landed on it when she'd been thrown.

And the terrible horse could smell her weakness.

She clutched the reins tightly, pressing her left hand into her thigh.

She wouldn't lose control of him again, wouldn't let him run.

Lily scratched a place on her side. Right where the binding was wrapped that currently hid her womanly figure.

Stella bit back the urge to correct her. She was well aware of how the binding constricted, how it made one sweat and itch.

"How long?" Lily said plaintively.

"Until we're safe." Stella pitched her voice in a lower register, completely dedicated to the farce they'd played since they'd reached Missouri.

"We ain't never gonna be safe again," came a muttered voice from inside the wagon.

Irene.

Lily sighed. With her hat pulled low like it was, Stella couldn't see the accompanying roll of her sister's eyes.

But she'd had charge of her sisters for almost a decade now, and she knew Lily. Lily had definitely rolled her eyes.

"We haven't seen anyone from outside our wagon train in two weeks," Stella reminded all three of them. She glanced around. There was no one within earshot. The closest wagon was several yards away and no one was on foot nearby.

If they wanted to keep up their ruse, they needed to be careful.

"The Byrne brothers ain't ones to give up so easy." Irene's statement held an ominous ring.

Over the past weeks, Stella had discovered that Irene was one of the most pessimistic people she'd ever known.

Other than herself, of course.

They'd traveled hundreds of miles from New York City, first by rail and then these past days by wagon train.

She hadn't realized the gravity of what she'd done. Not until it had been too late.

For nearly five weeks they'd been looking over their shoulders, jumping at every shadow.

She was tired.

And now the urgent feeling of danger had faded.

Irene continued to insist that the Byrne brothers wouldn't give up. She believed someone had been sent after them—the same man who'd chased them through a bustling Chicago train station.

But how could that man follow them out here? The prairie was wide open all around them.

And whoever he was, he would be looking for three sisters and a woman roughly fifteen years Stella's senior.

Not two brothers, a sister, and an elderly, sickly aunt.

If their disguises held—which they *should*—the Fairfax family, plus Irene, would reach the Willamette Valley in a few short months. They'd claim a homestead.

And be free.

Stella had been longing for that freedom since the crowded, dirty streets of New York City.

Longer. Since Dublin.

It was almost in her grasp. All she had to do was keep Irene calm, keep Lily from revealing her true identity, and keep them all safe.

All of which would be so much easier if Collin Spencer would leave her family alone.

She glanced over her shoulder to where the infuriating man walked alongside her sister Maddie. His horse trailed behind them. He held the reins loosely in his hands.

Maddie was speaking, though Stella couldn't read her lips. Not that it didn't stop her from trying.

Somewhere, a dog barked.

She would've felt even more secure in their plan if Maddie could've been disguised along with her and Lily. But unlike the two of them, Maddie's figure was too buxom to be bound and hidden.

Stella wished Maddie would stay in the wagon most of the time, like Irene did.

But Maddie had learned about healing herbs and basic first aid from a kindly neighbor during the hours that Stella had worked at the factory. And Maddie had such a tender heart that she couldn't leave someone sick or in pain if she could help.

Stella had to content herself with looking out for her sister.

Which would be much easier if Spencer left all of them alone.

The man was nosy as all get out. Stella had made the mistake of riding along with him and his twin brother on a hunt, and they'd peppered her with questions.

She'd been afraid she'd given herself away when she lost her lunch after skinning the buck they'd shot.

She was a city girl, born in Dublin. She bought her meat from a butcher. She'd never had to slaughter an animal before.

But she'd need to get used to it. There would be no grocers in Oregon.

Collin's voice drifted to her. She barely resisted the urge to turn in the saddle again. She'd *told* Maddie to act disinterested.

The man was certainly handsome enough to catch her sister's eye, but something about him made Stella's stomach twist uncomfortably when he was near.

He saw too much.

Their family couldn't afford for him to develop an interest in Maddie.

There was nothing more to it than that.

Maddie's lilting voice reached her ears next, and Stella couldn't resist looking.

But the stallion had anticipated her distraction. He reared and whinnied, nearly unseating her.

"Stella!" Lily cried.

There was no time to correct her sister for the slip up. Stella had to focus all her energy on staying in the saddle. Her right arm flared with pain as she gripped the horse's mane. Her thighs squeezed as she fought against the force of gravity.

And won.

Until a barking dog ran beneath the wagon wheels and

snapped at the stallion's foreleg. And from somewhere nearby, a sound like a gunshot.

The horse reared again. She lost control of the reins.

And the stallion bolted.

She clenched her teeth against the shriek that wanted to rip from her throat. She clung to the saddle horn with her left hand and the horse's mane with her right. The stallion's power unleashed. She could feel each stride lengthening beneath her as he galloped away from the wagon train.

A shout came from behind her. It sounded like Collin. Drat the man. He'd had his horse at hand—had he jumped into the saddle and followed her?

She forgot about him as she leaned low, trying to remain on the horse's back.

How was she to gain control of the horse without the reins? The horse was so tall she couldn't exactly reach forward to the bridle—not without chancing a fall that could kill her at this speed.

Rushing wind blew against her face and made tears stream from the corner of her eyes.

Fear knotted her stomach. Maddie and Lily needed her. She couldn't die.

All she had to do was stay on the horse. Eventually, he'd run himself out.

A gust of wind knocked her hat from her head. She didn't dare look back, especially when she felt her hair loose from the pins that usually held it secure. The blonde tresses unfurled behind her.

She could only pray Collin had been left far behind. The stallion must have some racehorse in his blood. He was fast.

But another shout came. Her stomach knotted.

She only saw the shallow trench in the landscape as the stallion's hooves left the ground.

She hadn't been prepared for him to leap, for the way her body would lift.

And then she was flying out of the saddle, falling, falling...

She tumbled and hit the ground with a sickening crunch.

"YOU BEEN DOIN' all right?" Collin Spencer asked Maddie.

The two of them walked side-by-side. He'd come straight from riding herd on the cattle and his horse walked behind the two of them, the reins in Collin's left hand keeping them tethered. Somewhere behind them among the snaking line of wagons was Collin's family. His twin brother, Coop. His older sister, Alice. And his older brother, Leo, who had very recently become engaged to another traveler, Evangeline Murphy. He was driving her wagon today. And probably mooning over her while he was at it.

"We're fine," Maddie said.

She didn't look fine. She looked bone-weary, with tiny lines fanning away from her eyes and a stiffness to her gait that spoke to exhaustion.

Collin hadn't realized they were going to be going so far today. It was getting on toward dark and the wagon train showed no signs of stopping. The nearest wagons— including the Fairfaxes'—continued to roll along, some of them creaking and groaning. Collin had found Maddie and asked her to go walking with him, like they'd planned days ago.

The mood in camp had been somber since Philip had been hanged for his crimes. Or maybe it was Collin himself, and not the entire wagon train, that had been changed somehow.

He'd known what could happen on a journey like this. Natural disasters, sickness, accidents.

He hadn't expected death to come so violently.

He shook the morose thoughts away.

Why was Hollis pushing them so hard today?

Maybe the wagonmaster was worried that they'd faced too many delays early in the journey. Collin'd heard talk of what could happen if they faced snow in the mountains ahead.

It was easier to think about what lay ahead than recent events, but Collin suddenly realized he wasn't being very good company.

"Is your aunt any better?" he asked politely.

Irene had grown ill again, remaining on bed rest in the wagon.

"I expect she'll be much recovered in a few days," Maddie said quietly.

She had her arms inside her shawl, the whole thing wrapped around her, hiding her upper body from view. Collin hadn't thought it was that cool this evening.

"Was it much warmer back home? You're from Ireland, right?" He thought someone had said that's where the family originated from. He could hear it in the lilting accent whenever Maddie spoke.

Maddie's lips pinched slightly. "It's not warm in Ireland."

She barely looked at him when she spoke, and he

couldn't help noticing she hadn't really answered his question. Collin didn't know whether she was incredibly shy or just didn't like him much.

He knew he couldn't keep up this ruse. He'd only asked her to come walking with him in the first place to give him more opportunity to spy on her family.

But he was done with that. Leo had found happiness with Evangeline. Collin was glad for his brother, really he was. Leo and Evangeline were going to get hitched the next time the wagon train stopped long enough to have a Sunday service.

But things had changed for Collin.

After everything that had happened the past few days, he didn't care anymore about ferreting out the Fairfax family's secrets. He'd only come walking tonight to let Maddie down easy.

He was needed in his own camp. Coop needed him, though he wasn't sure his brother would admit to it.

He and Coop always shared a special bond, but what'd happened back in New Jersey had created a rift in it.

Collin had thought time would make things right. Then Philip's hanging had scared him good.

If Coop didn't get his act together, they might not have time. Too much could go wrong on a journey like this.

So Coop needed him. Needed his attention. Alice, too, now that Leo was wrapped up in Evangeline.

Collin was done trying to figure out what was going on with the Fairfax family.

Maddie was acting kinda standoffish this evening. It'd probably be a relief to her that he wasn't going to bother her anymore.

And Stephen would be more than happy about that.

Maddie's brother was the conundrum that had piqued

Collin's interest. There was something the young man was hiding. The mystery of it had nettled Collin's curiosity.

Right now Stephen was riding his massive stallion, close by their family wagon that the younger brother, Louis, drove. Collin had slowed their steps so they'd fallen a bit behind the wagon and fanned out to one side. He and Maddie were close enough for the overprotective Stephen to keep an eye on them, but far enough for a little privacy.

In fact, Stephen had twisted in the saddle and was watching them right now.

It shouldn't matter that something about Stephen bugged him. Collin was going to let it go. He was.

But he couldn't seem to look away.

A dog barked, and Stephen's horse danced beneath him. The young man struggled for control, tightening his grip on the reins.

It didn't work.

A *bang*! rang out from somewhere nearby. Not a gunshot, but nearly as loud.

Collin jumped.

Stephen's stallion reared. The young man dropped the reins and lost control of the horse completely. He clung to the saddle, somehow stayed on the horse.

But then the horse bolted, heading out into the open prairie, away from the wagon train.

Collin reacted without a thought, turning to swing into his own saddle.

That horse was too big, too spirited for Stephen. The young man was going to get himself killed.

But not today if Collin could help it.

Maddie called out something behind him, but he didn't even look back as he urged his horse into a gallop. Collin's gelding wasn't as big as Stephen's stallion, but he was fast and he liked being given his head.

They raced after Stephen, flying over the uneven ground.

The stallion shook his head as he ran, trying to dislodge his rider without stopping to buck. He'd gone wild. Maybe he'd realized he was in control, that Stephen didn't have the reins and couldn't do anything to stop him.

"Jump off!" Collin shouted.

Somehow, Stephen stayed on. Maybe that was for the best.

If he fell now, with the horse at an outright canter, and didn't roll right, he'd break his neck.

Collin needed to get close enough to grab the reins. Or even to grab the man from the back of the horse.

Collin glanced over his shoulder. They'd already raced far enough away that the wagon train was out of sight. He'd hoped that maybe someone else had seen, that someone might come to help.

But the plains behind him were an empty stretch of prairie grass.

When he looked forward again, Stephen's hat flew off his head.

Blonde hair unfurled behind the man like a flag. *Long* blonde hair.

And then the stallion took a flying leap over what might be a small washout ahead—Collin didn't have a chance to see.

Because Stephen tumbled off the horse's back.

Heart in his throat, Collin reined in his horse.

The body was there, and as Collin hopped out of the saddle, he felt a bolt of relief to see Fairfax's chest rising and falling.

One step closer and Collin saw everything.

Blonde waves spilled around her shoulders like some fairytale character from a book. Without the hat usually hiding her face from view, elfin features. A splash of freckles across a nose.

Blue eyes flashed open, already glaring at Collin. For the first time, he got a good look at the sooty lashes surrounding them.

Stephen wasn't a young man at all.

Stephen was a woman.

TWO

Collin loomed over her. Stella coughed out a rattling breath.

Ignoring the spike of pain in her left side and his outstretched hand, she scrambled to her feet and backed away.

This was terrible.

He took a step toward her. She pushed past the pain in her right arm to dig into her hip pocket and produce the slender knife. She held it at the ready.

Collin went still as the silver blade gleamed between them, light glancing off its surface even as the sun slipped over the western horizon.

"Whoa," he said. "Take it easy." He held his hands out in front of him, as he would to calm an excitable pony.

"Get away from me," she spat.

His eyes flicked to her hip and back to her face. What was he—? She realized too late that she would've been better off pulling her gun on him.

Drat the man.

He didn't make any move to pull his gun on her.

"I just want to make sure you're all right," Collin said.

"I'm fine." The slight wheeze in her breath betrayed her. A nagging pain low in her left side meant she must've pulled something when she'd come off the stallion.

The stallion.

She whirled and could just make out his sleek black form galloping away, now almost out of sight at the horizon.

"Give me your horse," she demanded, turning back to Collin.

"Not likely." Something glittered in Collin's eyes. Amusement? Whatever it was, her stomach curdled like sour milk.

"Who are you? What's your name?"

She kept her knife at the ready and edged around him, keeping her body angled toward him all the while.

He quirked one eyebrow as she took a step back, toward where his horse stood. He'd left it vulnerable, its reins hanging down to the ground.

All she had to do was get closer and step up into the saddle.

"I'm sorry." How had it come to this? She'd been so careful to keep a low profile among the travelers.

Now she was threatening one of them with a knife.

She'd apologize again as soon as she got the stallion back.

Her mind was whirling chaos. Pain pulsed through her head with each beat of her heart. But it was imperative she retrieve the stallion. She couldn't think past that, couldn't think what she would do now that Collin Spencer knew her secret. How could she keep him quiet?

She'd lost her hat too. But that was another worry for later.

She took two more steps backward. Toward his horse.

The man hadn't moved. He stood with the setting sun now behind him, one hand on his hip.

She was almost there...

Collin whistled. A shrill *whee-ee* of two tones.

His horse *whuffled* and trotted past Stella to him.

She was so startled that she missed her opportunity to jump into the saddle or even grab the reins.

Collin took them in hand instead.

"How did you do that?" she demanded. She couldn't imagine the stallion responding like that no matter what she did.

"Practice," he said curtly. "Why don't you put your knife away and ask me for help?"

Anger at her hopeless situation rose to choke her. Tears burned behind her nose, but she ruthlessly stuffed them away. She never cried.

"I don't need your help," she ground out.

He raised one imperious eyebrow. She barely resisted the urge to shriek and stomp her foot.

She *hated* Collin Spencer.

"You're never going to track him down on foot—it's getting dark."

The man had a point.

"I guess you could head back to camp."

It would take hours to reach the wagon train on foot after the stallion had carried her such a far distance. They both knew it.

And that was if she didn't go astray in the darkness.

"I need my horse."

"You'd be better off without him," he said mildly. "He's too much horse for you."

Anger boiled in her belly. He was only saying that because he'd discovered she was a woman.

She forced her next words through gritted teeth. "Would you take me to find my horse?"

"Sure. As soon as you put away that knife."

He didn't want to take it from her?

"I've used it before," she warned him. It'd been years—she'd been all of seventeen when she'd had to defend herself—but she could still feel the way the teen boy's flesh had given way beneath the sharp edge of her knife, smell the metallic scent of blood.

She'd gotten away with her life, but barely.

Collin didn't blink. "Just don't use it on me."

He didn't sound frightened at all.

She wanted to frighten him a little. He was so big compared to her.

But the memory that had washed over her left her shaken. She slipped the knife into her pocket with trembling hands.

Collin had never threatened her. But he hadn't known she was a woman, either.

She needed to tread carefully. She needed to find the stallion. Once she did, she could put distance between herself and the terrible, nosy man.

The quicker that happened, the happier she'd be.

He swung up in the saddle. "You coming?" He stretched out his hand.

She stomped over to him and took it, allowing him to pull her into the saddle behind him.

"What's your name?" he asked again.

She stayed silent. Waited for him to get the horse moving.

Impatience flared when she realized he was waiting for her answer.

"Stephen," she said tartly. "My name is Stephen."

That's how it had to be until they reached Oregon.

He shook his head, but he must've known she wasn't going to give him more than that, because he urged the horse into a walk.

"Can't you push him harder?" she asked.

"It's dark."

It was true. Darkness had fallen around them. She could hear the chirping of crickets, the *whip-poor-will* of a bird. The air had chilled against her cheeks.

"Moon's almost full. It'll be up in another hour. We'll walk until then."

What if the stallion continued his gallop? They'd never catch up. She didn't know much about horses, only what the hostler in Independence had taught her in a fifteen-minute lesson. Could a horse like the stallion keep galloping as he had been for a long distance? She didn't know.

Impatience rankled. Lily and Maddie had witnessed both her and Collin ride off. If someone came after them and saw her hair unbound, it would be a disaster.

She didn't want to wait an hour to pick up speed. Didn't want to be close to Collin for any longer than she had to.

The only good thing about having to walk the horse meant she didn't need to hold onto him to keep her balance. Not at this pace.

She'd kept her distance in camp. This close, only inches away, he towered over her. He was at least a head taller. And she could feel every shift in his muscled back and shoulders as he moved easily with the horse. He had a grace on horseback that she couldn't aspire to.

And being close enough to feel every motion made her cheeks heat with awareness of him. Another thing to dislike him for.

———

"MAYBE OWEN WILL SEND A SEARCH PARTY," not-Stephen murmured after minutes of silence.

She wouldn't give him her name. But he knew it couldn't be Stephen.

"I don't know if he'll risk the manpower. And your sister saw me chase after you." Collin's heart pounded in his chest. It took an effort to make his voice even.

Now that he'd seen her without her hat, with her hair loose around her shoulders, he couldn't believe he'd ever thought not-Stephen a man. It was there in the dulcet tones of her voice. She always spoke quietly, pitched her voice low. But now that he knew, he couldn't hear a man when she spoke. Only her.

He felt foolish for only noticing now.

"Best we can hope for is to find that horse of yours quick and get back in the morning."

He felt her stiffen.

"What's the matter?"

"Nothing," she muttered.

He didn't believe her. "You running from something?"

She didn't answer, so he did it for her.

"Of course you are."

Still nothing.

He'd been suspicious before. Even told Coop about his

suspicions that there was something off about not-Stephen. But he'd never suspected *this*.

"You can trust me," he said when the silence lengthened between them. "My family can help you. What—or who—is it? Husband mistreating you?"

A harsh inhale from behind him. He wished it hadn't gotten dark, wished he could see her again.

That was a selfish wish. When he'd come upon her lying in the grass, he felt as if he'd stood too close to a powder explosion back at the mill. The very ground had rattled beneath his feet.

He'd never seen anyone so beautiful.

"Not a husband," he said when she stayed silent. "Someone threatening your siblings, then?"

"There's no need to talk," she snapped.

He could practically feel her vibrating with tension behind him. Couldn't forget the image of her wielding that knife, a wild fierceness in her expression that said she meant business.

But why hadn't she pulled the gun on him, if she was afraid? It didn't make sense.

"We might as well," he said. "Nothing else to do to pass the time."

The moon was coming up. He could see a faint glow on the horizon. It would light their way and hopefully help them catch up to her stallion.

"Where'd you get that horse anyway? He's not right for you."

She growled low in her throat. It made him think of Alice on the rare occasions she got angry. Both women reminded him of a kitten who'd gotten riled up—neither one had claws big enough to do much damage.

It was kinda cute.

He didn't think not-Stephen would appreciate that thought, so he kept it to himself.

"He'll be the start of a good breeding program once we get to Oregon," she said tightly.

"*If* you get him to Oregon."

He could imagine her pique. Felt her holding her breath.

"You'd do better to sell him to someone at one of the forts," he suggested. "Use the money for some other kind of business venture."

"I don't want to sell him."

"You're like to get yourself killed trying to ride him. You could've broken your neck earlier."

"I'll thank you to mind your own business," she said coldly.

There was something about the tone of her voice that reminded him of his twin. Coop hated being told what to do—or that he couldn't do something. If anything, it made him more determined to do what he shouldn't.

Coop was the most stubborn man on the planet. And Collin loved him.

Collin had been shocked to discover not-Stephen was a woman, and maybe his shock had contributed to him trying to tell her what to do, trying to get her to accept his help.

But his instant realization that she might be more like Coop than Alice made him go quiet.

If it was true, then he'd have to do what he did with Coop. Lead him in a roundabout way to the right path. Let him think it was his idea. And hopefully keep him from getting himself killed.

Coop was difficult. More so in the past months.

Collin could only hope that not-Stephen was less stubborn than his brother. Collin was a patient man. The fear she'd exhibited brought out his protective side.

Whatever she was running from, it had to be serious. Why else would she have embarked on a two-thousand-mile journey across the wilderness to escape it? Hiding her true identity had to be hard.

If he could prove to her that he could be trusted, he could help her.

And that meant the first thing he needed to do was find her horse. Convincing her to give up the beast could come later.

The moon emerged over the horizon, bathing the prairie around them in soft golden light. There was a wild beauty about the landscape. Shadows cast by little rises, scrub bushes, dips in the land.

He pushed the gelding into a lope, felt a thrill when not-Stephen's hands gripped his waist. He followed where he'd seen her stallion disappear over the horizon. It was too dark to read any sign or tracks on the ground. He was trusting his gut.

Not-Stephen seemed to relax a bit as they covered more ground. Or maybe she'd relaxed because Collin wasn't speaking.

He slowed his horse to a walk when they neared a winding creek. He reined in, pointed to the tracks on the bank. Her stallion had stood here for a bit, moved in a circle. Probably drank from the creek.

He let his gelding have a good drink while he scanned the horizon in all directions. The stallion had stopped, and that was a good thing. But where had he gone? He was a cagey animal. Smart.

Not a wild animal, but not keen to go back to not-Stephen.

Collin wheeled his horse and let the animal splash into the creek, move downstream at a slow pace.

"What are you doing?" not-Stephen asked.

Maybe she didn't realize she still gripped the sides of his shirt with both hands.

"I've got a hunch."

They followed the creek for several quiet minutes, until he reined in, stopping the gelding.

Not-Stephen leaned around him, her arm brushing his elbow. Awareness skittered up his spine.

There was the stallion, a darker shadow against the landscape. He was grazing at the edge of the creek, not far ahead.

"Let me down," she ordered, her voice not much louder than a whisper.

"Wait a second. Let's make a plan—"

She didn't wait. She swung her leg over his gelding's back and dropped, splashing loudly into the creek, dangerously close to his horse's back hooves. Before he could stop her, she'd taken the rope he'd had secured to his saddle.

Collin bit back a curse and steadied his horse with a hand on its neck.

"He's going to bolt again," he warned her. "He's got a taste of freedom."

She clearly didn't want his help, because she marched out of the water, straight toward the still-saddled and bridled stallion.

"All right, partner," she said, her voice sweet and sugary. She shook out the rope, making a loop. Not a very good one.

Collin shook his head. Her form was awful. That rope wasn't going to make it around the horse's neck.

"You've had your fun, now it's time—" She hadn't got

close enough, barely started twirling her loop, before the stallion trotted away.

And Collin didn't feel elation at being right. He just felt tired. Every day on the wagon train was a slog of hard work. His family had invested most of Leo and Alice's inheritance from their estranged father into a herd of cattle. Collin spent the days either herding the animals in a general westward direction or driving the wagon.

He'd put in a full day today. He wanted his bedroll. His stomach grumbled.

And now not-Stephen wasn't cooperating.

He forced himself to take a deep breath. Think of Coop. Have patience.

The stallion didn't go far. It was probably tired, too. After several yards, it slowed and then stood, lowering its head to graze again.

Not-Stephen stood where she was, her shoulders set, not looking back at Collin.

"Do you want my help?" Collin asked.

"No," she answered fiercely.

Fine.

All the patience he'd told himself to practice dissipated.

He wheeled his horse and moved up on the opposite bank. Found a flat place not far away and dismounted. He didn't have his bedroll. That was back at camp, in the wagon. But he unsaddled his horse anyway. The gelding was easily ground tied and Collin settled himself on the grass, using his saddle for his pillow.

"What are you doing?" From this distance, her voice sounded scandalized, or angry, or both.

"It's late. I'm going to catch a few hours of rest before I head back toward camp in the morning." He could only hope Leo wasn't out here somewhere, tracking him down. His brother could be too protective sometimes.

Collin pulled his hat low over his face, blocking out most of the moonlight.

If not-Stephen wanted to chase that stallion around all night, she was on her own.

But he wasn't leaving her out here by herself.

THREE

Collin woke as the first rays of dawn were crashing over the horizon. The little creek burbled softly and some kind of bird whistled shrill notes.

When he pushed his hat back on his head and sat up to stretch, he caught sight of not-Stephen sitting on the creekbank. The same side as him.

Not-Stephen had her arms wrapped around her bent knees. She looked small and alone.

It only lasted a second. Then she registered that he was awake and stiffened, her arms falling to her sides.

The stallion was minding his own business on the other side of the creek. It was telling that he hadn't wandered off, though. He'd stayed close. He didn't really want to be on his own, or he would've kept going, even with the saddle and bridle on.

"Morning," Collin said, voice rough with sleep.

"You were right." It wasn't the greeting he'd expected, and her words were spoken with a bitter tone.

He didn't feel any satisfaction. And he already knew it.

He hadn't fallen into a deep sleep last night, not while she'd huffed and puffed as she had chased the stallion back and forth late into the night. He'd been too aware of her movements, the cadence of her voice, to sleep fully. He was also conscious that someone who had pulled a knife on him might sneak up and try and steal his gelding in the night—although he'd figured she was too smart for that. If she showed up back in camp with his horse and no Collin, she was liable to get herself in a heap of trouble.

He rubbed a tired hand down his face. His stomach was growling, a reminder that he hadn't had supper last night and that he was going to miss breakfast this morning.

"Do you want my help?" he asked.

"No."

He'd already let his eyes wander over to the stallion, formulating his plan. But now his gaze darted back toward her.

She still didn't look at him. "But apparently, I need it."

He didn't gloat. He just stood up and put the saddle on his gelding, who was grazing contentedly nearby. Got his horse bridled up and ready to ride.

He moved toward not-Stephen. She had the rope coiled by her side and was flipping her closed knife over and over in her fingers.

"You figuring on using that this morning?" He stopped a couple feet away.

She frowned. "Not on you." She reached out to fiddle with the end of her hair, her frown growing fierce. "I lost my hat."

He didn't see what that had to do with the knife.

She must've sensed his confusion because she turned her frown on him. "If I ride back to camp like this, I'll be discovered."

Ah. That. He'd been so thoroughly shocked last night... and then had grown used to knowing her secret. He'd forgotten he was the only one who did.

"I should just cut it all off." But the way she said the words, the reluctance in her tone, he knew she didn't want to.

"You can do it later. After we charm your friend over there." He stepped closer and extended his hand to help her up.

Standing beside her with her squinting up at him, the growing sunlight gilded her hair and the tips of her eyelashes gold. Even with her suspicious squint, he hadn't seen a prettier sight.

She took his hand. He pulled her upright.

"Thank you," she murmured. She dusted off her trousers and then bent to pick up the coil of rope.

"You hang onto it," he said when she tried to hand it to him. "You sure you need to stay disguised?" Before she answered, he started off toward the creek and the stallion on the other side of it, walking slowly. His stomach was grumbling again. He sure missed Alice's biscuits and gravy this morning.

When she still didn't answer, he glanced sideways at her. "It can't be that bad."

She cleared her throat. "A coupla men chased us by train from New York City to Chicago."

"What'd you do?" It was the wrong question, and he knew it as soon as he spoke.

She bristled, staring off into the bright sunlight.

"Never mind."

It was more information than she had given him last night. It wasn't enough for him to know how to help her, but he wanted to keep her talking.

"Where'd you learn to ride? Who taught you?" He had been wondering since last night.

She seemed relieved for the subject change. "I taught myself, I guess."

"What's that mean?"

"I never rode a horse before him."

She had to be kidding. When he'd thought her a man, he had noticed how awkward she seemed. But if she was telling the truth, it was no wonder she'd been having such a difficult time.

"You got any information about that horse? What did the man who sold him to you say about him?"

"What does that have to do with taming him?" she asked sharply.

"I figure he's what... Three or four years old?"

She shrugged.

"He had a life before you bought him. Whoever had him before, fed him, took care of him... Whoever that was, they taught him what it was like to partner with a human. If they weren't a very good teacher, then you might be suffering for it."

"Are you saying the hostler in Independence sold me a defective horse?"

He couldn't help smiling, but when she grew perturbed, he tried to stifle it.

"No. I'm saying that maybe he had a bad teacher. But now he has you."

She looked doubtful. "I'm his teacher?"

"That's right. Don't worry. I'll help you get started."

The horse lifted his head when not-Stephen stepped into the water. She leveled a look on Collin and then she hung back as he crossed the creek. He didn't argue with her.

He stuck one hand into his pocket, fishing for what he'd stashed there yesterday—though it seemed like ages ago now. When he climbed to the top of the creekbank, he stood still.

And waited.

The sun kept climbing, bathing the prairie in pink and orange and gold. And kept on climbing, until the magical early-morning stillness ended. A bird chattered from nearby. A rabbit hopped away. The breeze kicked up.

The stallion snuffled. Collin held his hand outstretched, offering the treat he'd put in his pocket for the gelding yesterday.

The stallion took one step toward him. Then another.

He heard not-Stephen whisper something from behind him but didn't twitch a muscle. The stallion kept coming. And then lipped the peppermint candy out of his palm.

STELLA FELT a curious mix of relief and frustration as the stallion she'd spent hours pursuing last night walked right up to Collin.

"Would you bring me the rope?" Collin asked, voice calm and low.

Stella pulled a face and silently mimed his question as she slogged through the water around her ankles. She was fetching and carrying for him now, was she?

She was only grumpy because she was exhausted. She'd been far more aware of every noise in the night out here with just Collin than back at camp surrounded by other people. She had only drifted off a couple of times.

Not only was she tired, she was worried.

Were her sisters all right?

Was coming West like this the right decision?

What was she going to do about her hair?

She came out of the shallow creek and approached man and horse warily. Collin was speaking to the horse in a low tone, his words inaudible. He had one hand on the reins and the other on the horse's neck.

When she came up behind Collin, the stallion bobbed its head.

Collin dropped the reins.

"What are you doing?" she hissed. Thinking about chasing the stallion across the countryside all over again made her want to cry.

And that made her angry.

"Easy." Collin's command was gentle. Stella wanted to punch him.

But the stallion quieted.

Collin reached back with one hand.

She pressed the coiled rope into his palm with more force than was necessary. "Of course he likes you," she muttered. "You bribed him."

"It's not a bribe," Collin said. The stallion stood while Collin formed the rope into a loop and while Collin slipped the loop over his head. The man wasn't even holding onto the end of the rope. It was laid over his shoulder and trailed down to the ground.

"Think of it like this." Collin began unbuckling the bridle at the side of the horse's long muzzle. "I worked at a powder mill before my family made this journey. I worked all day long and when I was finished, I got paid. Man or animal, we deserve to be paid for our work."

"And a treat from your pocket is like a payment?" She couldn't keep the skepticism from her voice. She hadn't even seen what he'd used. Some kind of candy, maybe?

"Why not? I want him to work with me, don't I?"

He slipped the bridle over the horse's ears and off.

"Don't berate me just yet," Collin said. He hadn't even turned his head to look at her, but somehow he knew she'd opened her mouth to question him.

"I think you've got something wrong with his bit. Here, you see?" Collin held up the bridle and there was a flash of red against the silver metal. "He's cut himself on it somehow."

Compassion swelled and her breath stuck in her chest. "I didn't even know that could happen. Will he be all right?"

"His mouth should heal in a few days."

A few days. What was she supposed to do until then? How was she to ride him back to the wagon train?

Collin was doing something with the rope. He'd moved the loop higher on the horse's head, behind the stallion's ears like a bridle would be. He made another loop.

"I can feel how hard you're thinking," Collin said. "And he can, too." He nodded to the horse in front of him. "Horses are intelligent animals. They can sense when you're upset. Or anxious. Frightened."

She almost choked on the burble of near-hysterical laughter that bubbled up inside her. If what Collin said was true, the stallion hadn't known a moment of peace with Stella on his back. How could she put aside the fear when she was being pursued by terrifying, dangerous men? Trying to keep up a facade for her sisters?

Collin took a half-step back, admiring his handiwork. He'd somehow fashioned the rope into a halter of sorts. "It's called a hackamore. It will hold until we get back to camp. I hope."

It would be like holding a cloud, she imagined. If the

stallion got a wild idea to race across the plains again, a simple rope wrapped around his muzzle would give her absolutely no control.

"Hey."

She hadn't realized he was looking at her. She turned startled eyes on him. He was big and maddeningly calm. His gaze was frank and assessing.

She cut her eyes away, unable to bear it.

Something warm slipped over the crown of her head, fitting snugly just above her ears. Her eyes were suddenly shaded from the bright morning sunlight.

He'd put his hat on her.

She tipped her head so she could see him.

"Don't cut your hair," he said gruffly.

Her chin lifted, her stubborn nature piqued at being told what to do.

His lips twitched, as if he knew her thoughts.

He tipped his head toward the stallion. "You ready?"

She wasn't, but she nodded.

Collin slipped something into her palm. A piece of dried apple. The stallion must've followed the movement, because he was already dipping his head to take the treat from her hand.

As always, she was the tiniest bit overwhelmed by his massive size. It was never more noticeable than when they were close.

"Don't tense up," Collin whispered.

She ignored him and took a half-step closer to the horse, laying her empty palm on his neck the way she'd seen Collin do not long ago.

"What's his name?" Collin asked. "I've been calling him Beast in my head."

"I don't know his name. The hostler never told me."

She was beginning to think she'd been swindled. Not that she could regret it now. It was over and done.

"A horse needs a name." Collin had moved to the opposite side of the stallion, barely able to see over the animal's back.

She kept her hand on the horse's neck. Tried to feel something. Was she supposed to be able to feel his heartbeat? Speak to him silently? How did Collin calm him? It couldn't only be the treat in his pocket.

"Breathe in deeply," Collin said. His voice was low and warm.

She only followed his instructions because she wanted to get back to camp.

"Feel how peaceful it is this morning."

Her eyes closed of their own accord as she breathed in the sweet scent of dew and long prairie grasses.

She didn't have to cut her hair. That thought crept in and stuck like a burr to her pant leg.

She should have cut it ages ago. Before they'd left Independence. But she hadn't, choosing instead to hide it beneath her hat with pins to keep it up and out of the way.

She could still cut it. She would, if it meant keeping her sisters safe.

But she didn't have to make that decision this morning. Because Collin had plopped his hat on her head.

She glanced up at him. The sun was sitting just over his shoulder, turning the ends of his brown hair gold, hair that was matted and rumpled from his hat.

He wasn't smiling, though he usually smiled all the time. She'd noticed it about him. Yet still it was lurking there, at the corners of his mouth, ready to bloom into a full-fledged smirk or grin.

Her stomach did a slow flip.

She'd treated him abominably when he'd only tried to help her.

She didn't want his help, but she'd needed it last night and this morning.

Something shifted inside her.

She owed him. But it was more than that.

She cleared her throat. "My name is Stella."

FOUR

My name is Stella.

Collin couldn't stop thinking about her, even though he was supposed to be counting the heads of his family's cattle as the day drew to a close.

The cows were restless this evening, bunched up and milling around. What was bugging them?

His stomach roared with hunger, and he hadn't wanted his bedroll this desperately in weeks. Mid-morning, he and Stella—disguised again as Stephen, though he'd never see her that way again—had ridden straight into a search party of six men, though the party had only made it a half mile from the already-moving wagon train.

His brother Leo had been one of the men riding out to find them, and Collin had instantly seen the lines of stress and worry around his brother's eyes. Coop was usually the one to make Leo worry like that.

The other men had circled around them, making Stella's stallion dance nervously. Collin had sidled closer to her, which seemed to calm the stallion a bit. When she'd hesitated, he'd quickly explained how they'd been stranded overnight but gotten the stallion back.

The last he'd seen of Stella she was riding toward her family's wagon. She hadn't looked back.

But that hadn't stopped him thinking about her while Alice had plied him with a thick slice of fried ham and pan cornbread. As he'd shoveled the food into his gullet, he'd wondered what Stella was eating.

After Leo'd shooed him off to watch over the cattle, Collin wondered if she'd tied up the stallion and was driving the wagon. Had her family been worried about her?

Was she going to tell them that Collin knew the big secret?

His wandering thoughts meant he lost count again, and he bit back a groan.

Coop waved the *all-clear* sign from the other side of the herd. He started riding around the outer edge of the cattle. Collin went to meet him.

"They sure are riled up tonight."

Coop shifted his shoulders. "I thought you'd be more riled up after being stuck with that doofus all night long."

Collin kept his expression neutral. "He's not so bad."

"Whoa ho," Coop scoffed. "You've changed your mind about him? What happened to your certainty that he was up to no good?"

Collin reined in his temper. He had only himself to blame for this conversation. He was the one who had spent the last two weeks telling Coop all his suspicions about Stella.

Suspicions that had turned out to be correct. But he couldn't tell his brother, couldn't break Stella's confidence.

"Stephen is a city slicker. Out of his element. If I saw anything strange in his behavior, that's all it was." He needed to distract his brother from the topic. "I really need to catch a few hours of shut-eye before I take a turn on watch. Leo wanted me on first watch, but I don't think I can do it. Can you swap me?"

Coop grunted. Was that supposed to be a yes or no?

"What?" Collin prompted.

"I guess I can swap. I was going to play cards with a couple of friends."

Collin felt as if he'd been stabbed in the stomach with a fiery hot poker.

Coop's irresponsibility had cost Collin and Leo their jobs in New Jersey and sent the entire family on this journey.

And now he wanted to *play cards?*

Collin had to swallow back his ire before he could pitch his voice in a tone that wouldn't put his brother's back up. "I thought you were going to clean up your act."

Coop bristled. Collin had known he would. But the words just wouldn't stay inside.

"You're as much a stick in the mud as Leo," Coop said.

"No, I'm not. You shouldn't be gambling."

Coop's mouth twisted. "I gave up drinking. There's no harm in having a little fun. That's all it is. Having fun."

Collin carefully kept his face blank. Anything he said now was going to irritate his brother further.

Coop claimed he wasn't going to drink alcohol anymore. That was well and good. But what if his card-playing buddies decided to have a drink? Would he really be able to abstain?

Coop had always done what he wanted, whether it was against the rules or not.

Leo wasn't going to like this. But should he even tell his brother? Leo and Evangeline had been through a lot recently. Hollis thought the wagon train would have a day of rest in another two days, and Leo and Evangeline planned to get married then. Worrying about Coop was the last thing Leo needed.

"Do you want my help or not?" Coop's resentful question sparked little prickles all along Collin's skin.

But he made himself smile. "Thanks, brother. I appreciate your help."

Yip yip yip.

Both brothers' heads turned toward the sound echoing over the ridge in the distance.

"Coyotes," Coop said.

"That must be what's got the cattle riled." Collin listened to the sound, a cacophony of canine voices. Would Leo want them both on watch if there were critters about?

"I can hear your stomach grumbling from here," Coop said. "You better head back to camp and grab some dinner and your bedroll."

Collin didn't like leaving things with his brother like this, with this tension between them.

But Coop was right, and there was more work to be done tomorrow.

In camp, Alice handed him a bowl of stew. He brought it with him as he unrolled his bedroll near the wagon.

Leo was seated near the fire cuddling Evangeline's daughter, Sara, while making lovey-dovey eyes at Evangeline, who was working with Alice to clean up.

Something tugged around Collin's neck. He reached up to loosen the leather cord he always wore beneath his shirt. The cord kept his mother's wedding ring tied closely around his neck. He rubbed the simple silver band between his thumb and finger as he watched Leo and Evie.

Collin had a faint memory of his pa looking at Ma the very same way.

Pa would've known how to handle Coop.

Collin thought of Stella again, how she'd reacted so similarly to his twin. Tell either of them outright what to do and they balked.

He needed to stay two steps ahead of Coop. Playing cards was a distraction. Something to break up the monotony of the journey. Collin could make other kinds of fun. Hadn't they had a good time when they'd played music and gotten everyone nearby to dance and sing with them?

No reason they couldn't do that again.

Maybe even after Leo's wedding. The beginnings of his plan came together but weariness overtook him as he finished his supper.

He finally curled into his bedroll and dropped off to sleep.

"I STILL DON'T UNDERSTAND why we can't just tell everyone who we really are."

Stella shook her head at Lily's statement. She was stoking the fire while Lily chopped up some venison on the tailgate of the wagon not far away.

In camp, they always made a stack of crates as a sort of a barrier to keep them a little bit separate from the rest of camp.

Tonight, even that felt different. Collin could walk right over and announce to everyone that she was a woman.

Why hadn't she made him promise that he'd keep her secret?

"He didn't make a big fuss out of it," Lily complained further.

The fire crackled. Stella pushed another small stick into the growing flame. "I didn't say that. He was surprised." She might never forget the shock on his face when he'd seen her with her hair loose. "And maybe he didn't get angry, but that doesn't mean other people won't. People don't like to be duped."

Lily growled a little in her throat. "I told you this was a bad idea from the beginning."

It was true. Lily had argued that there had to be a better way. Stella had suspected it was mostly because she didn't want to dress the part of a man.

Back in Dublin, Stella had dressed like a man since she was sixteen and realized she needed to go to work in the factory or her sisters would starve. She'd been young, frightened of what could happen to a young woman on her own. She'd made the best choice that she could, and it had served her well.

"It won't be forever," she told her sister.

Lily harrumphed and ducked her head down.

He wasn't angry.

Collin hadn't been angry, though she had expected it. It's why she had drawn her knife on him.

She was trying to forget the whole ordeal had even happened, but snatches of thoughts of the man kept sneaking in while she'd driven the wagon and made camp today.

Especially when she ground tied the stallion for the night. She couldn't stop remembering Collin and that candy. Where was she supposed to get a supply of candy? Maybe at the fort in a few days, but the expense felt frivolous when they still had to cross half the continent.

"How am I supposed to find a husband dressed like this?" Lily murmured. Stella didn't know if it was meant for her or just a complaint to herself.

She answered anyway. "The Good Lord will provide you a husband when he's ready for you to have one."

To her mind, Lily was still too immature to make a good wife.

But no one could argue that Lily could cook. If her husband could be won through his belly, Lily would certainly win his affections.

"Maddie doesn't want a husband, and neither do you, but I'm the one stuck in this awful boy's garb."

It was true. Maddie had been saying since she was old enough to understand relationships that she didn't want to marry. But—

"I never said I didn't want a husband," Stella said, with a furtive glance around to make sure no one was within earshot.

"You sure don't act like it," Lily said.

A sharp retort was on the tip of Stella's tongue. Did Lily really imagine she wanted to dress this way, too?

She'd done what needed doing back home in Ireland, and she was still doing it.

Father had worked in the factory for as long as she could remember. Mother had died when Maddie had been seven or eight. Stella had been ten. Father had disappeared into a bottle after that. He'd disappeared further and further, until Stella had been forced to do things she wasn't proud of to try and survive.

He'd wasted away and died when she was sixteen. Stella had done everything she could to keep her sisters from being forced out onto the street.

She was used to making the sacrifice. And she knew her sisters were grateful.

Lily was just having a moment. She was probably still frightened for Stella. When Stella had ridden into camp, both of her sisters' relief had been palpable.

Evangeline Murphy's father had died in a violent outburst at the hands of another traveler. Maddie had been doctoring wounds and sicknesses all along the journey. They all three knew how quickly something could go wrong.

But Stella was all right, and she intended to keep things that way.

Just then, Irene hustled into camp. She and Maddie had gone to visit a nearby creek to wash up.

Irene was only ten years Stella's senior, but she had lived a hard life, and it showed. She could pass for someone twenty-five years older than Stella.

On this journey, she had been using that to her advantage, keeping herself wrapped in a bulky shawl and using a walking stick. But somehow tonight she'd forgotten to make herself look slow and sickly as she hustled into camp. Her eyes were wild.

"What's the matter?" Stella asked.

"Where's Maddie?" Lily asked.

"I saw him. He was talking to Hollis—"

The rest of Irene's words were garbled and muffled by the wagon canvas as she ducked inside

"Saw who?" Lily asked, looking as confused as Stella felt.

Maddie appeared, one hand holding the small towel she had taken with her and the other the bar of lye soap.

"What is Irene talking about?" Stella demanded of her middle sister.

"We were walking back from the creek when she saw a stranger speaking to Hollis." Maddie kept her voice low. "She swears it's one of the Byrnes' men."

There was silence from inside the wagon now. Like Irene thought if she didn't even breathe, no one would find her.

Stella felt for the gun at her hip. She'd never used one before. Maybe Collin had figured it out.

Collin. Maybe...

She shook thoughts of the man away. She didn't need help.

"I'll take a walk around camp," she said.

It'd been the same faces since day one. Over a hundred in their company and two other companies in the wagon train besides. Maybe Irene had been mistaken. Maybe it was a traveler from one of the other companies. Irene had been hiding in the wagon enough that she couldn't know all the faces. Not like Stella did, with her constant watchfulness.

"Are you sure?"

"Be careful."

Lily and Maddie's words overlapped.

Stella firmed her chin. She would've liked to hug her sisters, offer comfort at a moment like this. But she didn't know who was watching, and she didn't want to arouse suspicion.

She made a slow circuit around camp on foot.

Nobody spoke to her. Everyone was busy.

Mothers caring for their small children.

A group of three men smoking pipes and conversing.

A boy of about ten playing with his dog.

Stella was separate from it all, even as she walked

through the busy camp. No one called out to her. No one motioned her to join them.

It was the way it had to be. But her chest felt a little hollow anyway.

She saw nothing out of the ordinary. She recognized everyone.

There was Hollis, chatting with Owen near the Spencer wagon.

Leo and Evangeline sat near their campfire, heads together.

Collin was nowhere to be seen. Wait—there was a dark head emerging from a bedroll near their wagon. It had to be him.

She resolutely averted her gaze.

It was too risky to make another loop through the camp. Someone would notice her for sure. And she hadn't spotted any strange men.

Maybe Irene was mistaken.

But what if she wasn't?

Stella was so tired she wanted to cry, but if there was a chance Irene had really seen someone sent by the Byrne brothers, she would need to stay on watch.

FIVE

A day off from the relentless roll of the wagon wheels.

Stella had spent the past two days feeling as if she were slogging through molasses. Half-terrified and half-angry. She stayed constantly alert, ready to defend her sisters against the man Irene continued to insist worked for the Byrne brothers.

Irene hadn't come out of the wagon since his arrival in camp.

Stella had insisted Maddie and Lily stay close, and for once, they hadn't argued. Yesterday, late in the afternoon, she'd seen a rider she hadn't recognized from their company. It was only from a distance, and he'd been in profile to her as he spoke to a man in another wagon. With his dark vest over dark trousers and bowler hat pulled low over his face, she hadn't been able to make him out clearly.

They'd been in New York City for such a short time. Only a matter of weeks. All three of them living in a room no bigger than a hatbox. The faces of the people who'd lived in the same tenement apartment building had blurred together.

She only knew most of her neighbors by the weary hopelessness of their bowed shoulders and eyes that had shown how clearly they'd given up.

She didn't know that she could pick out one of the men who worked for the Byrne brothers from a crowd, but Irene continued to insist in whispers that the mysterious man in camp was one of them. That he'd have no mercy on them.

She never should've done what she'd done. Stolen from the Byrne brothers. But back in New York City, she'd believed Irene when she'd insisted they would get away scot-free.

Technically, Stella had stolen *back* what had been taken from her. She'd believed she was righting a wrong.

Irene had helped her, eager to escape herself.

Stella hadn't known that the Byrne brothers would send someone after them, would want to kill her and her sisters just for escaping their evil clutches.

If this henchman discovered them, it would be disastrous.

And now they had an entire day stuck in camp. Inside the ring of wagons, surrounded by nosy neighbors, she felt trapped.

But with only the one horse between them, there was no quick getaway to be had. Where would they go? There were no homes out here. Nowhere to hide.

It was early yet, but Stella had rousted herself from her bedroll beneath the wagon long ago. She couldn't afford to sleep, couldn't afford a lazy morning. It was up to her to protect her sisters. No one else would.

She walked the stallion away from camp, a simple loop

over his neck. Working with the horse gave her an excuse to be awake and moving around this early, while mist still rose from the prairie grasses and the sky was still purple and orange as the sun rose.

She'd had to untie Collin's rope bridle that first night, and she couldn't figure out how he'd made the knots to hold to put it back again. She'd settled for tying a rope around the stallion's neck and letting him walk along behind the wagon these past two days, bribing the horse with pinches of sugar from Lily's small barrel in the wagon. But there was no calm to be found inside her. She felt as spooked as a horse surrounded by a pack of wolves.

A man strode around the outside edges of the circled wagons, the only movement to be seen at the quiet camp.

Stella tensed, moved so that the horse was at her back. He was a formidable size. Some of the people in camp avoided him because of his unpredictable nature.

The man's features came into sharp focus as the sun slipped over the horizon. It was Collin. She wilted in relief, though she hid it by turning her shoulder to him. Her fingers fumbled with the rope.

"Morning," he said easily as he approached, his boots rustling in the late-spring grasses.

She nodded tightly. On the heels of her relief came frustration that changed quickly into a flash of anger.

Collin was a risk. He knew her secret, and if he wasn't careful, he might be the reason she was found out.

"You haven't told anyone—about me, have you?" She tried her best to make the words sound casual.

Collin must've heard her consternation anyway. He went still, gazing at the stallion grazing just behind her. "Why would I?"

Her knot was all wrong and she picked at the rope,

trying to untangle it. "We never made an agreement, before we came back to camp." It'd been on the tip of her tongue to say something just as they'd ridden into the group of riders who'd been searching for them.

"There's no need for an agreement. I won't tell anyone."

She kept her eyes on the rope between her fingers. It wouldn't come undone. It wasn't as if she could force him into silence. And that loss of control made her feel even worse.

She was more tangled up inside than this silly knot.

The camp was waking up now, movement inside the ring of wagons. Her attention was distracted from the man beside her as she squinted to try and see that no one was approaching her wagon.

"You're making it worse." Collin's voice was mild, but he'd taken a step closer. His hand closed over hers on the knot.

She jumped, jerking away from his touch. The rope dropped to the ground. The stallion made a low nicker and took two steps away.

"Hey." Collin held his hands out at his sides. He was bareheaded—because she still wore his hat. It made it too easy to see his eyes, and the concern inside them. "What's the matter?"

She struggled to gain control of her breath, which wanted to come too rapidly. "Nothing." She ducked her head, then bent to pick up the rope she'd dropped. "It's nothing. Just this knot."

She felt his gaze on her, felt him watching her for a beat too long. "Can I help?"

She tossed the end of the rope to him, somehow knowing that he wasn't going to leave her alone.

It only took him a second to unravel the knot she hadn't been able to. "It's easier without gloves on," he said simply.

She rarely took her gloves off. Her hands were small. A woman's hands. Wearing the gloves was safer. She didn't tell him that.

"Are you trying to make the hackamore again? I can show you."

A hackamore. Maybe if she let him help with this, he would leave her alone. She felt the beat of her heart in the lobes of her ears as her eyes flicked back to camp. Lily, dressed as Louis, was tending the fire near their wagon now.

She thought Collin would tie the rope into a halter again, but he handed her the rope. He instructed her, patient when she flipped her wrist the wrong way and had to start over.

He didn't stand too close—but it didn't matter. She was aware of the breadth of his shoulders; the strong line of his jaw, scruffy with stubble; his large hands compared to hers.

"Good work," he praised when she slipped the rope over the stallion's head. "You named him yet?"

She shook her head.

He'd done what he'd come for. Helped her. Checked on her. Would he leave now?

He didn't. "My brother's getting married this morning."

She'd forgotten about that. The company had planned a worship service since they wouldn't be traveling today. And word of mouth spread through camp that everyone was invited to the wedding of two of their own.

Everyone gathered together might put her and Lily and Maddie in danger.

She worked to keep her face neutral. Collin saw too much.

"You need any more help, I'll be around," he said.

She nodded. She wouldn't ask him for help and they both knew it.

He rose on the tips of his toes as if to start walking, but then settled again. "'Specially if you want some shooting lessons."

Her gaze darted to him. He was watching her with an inscrutable expression.

"The more I thought about it, I realized there must be a reason you didn't pull your gun on me out there when you thought I was a threat."

She should've. He was more threat to her right now than anyone else, wasn't he?

"You can't shoot, can you?" he prodded.

"I've got a gun, haven't I?" She gave a light tug on the stallion's rope. If Collin wouldn't leave, she would.

"Doesn't mean you can use it," he called after her quietly.

She knew the mechanics of it. But the weight of the revolver at her hip was heavy as she walked back toward camp.

Almost as heavy as the worry for what would happen if they were discovered.

LEO HAD ASKED Collin to stand up with him during the wedding ceremony.

Just after the worship service concluded, they joined Hollis, who was acting preacher, at the front of the crowd.

Leo wore his nicest shirt and had spent ten minutes carefully brushing trail dust off his pants this morning.

Evangeline wore a pale yellow dress that heightened the roses in her cheeks. Her hair was up in a fancy twist that Collin had only seen once before.

Evangeline had asked Alice to stand by her side, and she held her young sister by the hand. Sara couldn't be more than three, but Evangeline doted on her. And now that Evangeline was all Sara had left, she would be both mother-figure and big sister.

Had Leo felt that responsibility when he'd been left with charge of the three of them? He'd been younger than Evangeline, only fifteen when Ma had died and everything changed. He'd worked for the powder mill longer than that.

Leo deserved his happiness. He faced Evangeline, clasping her hands in his as Alice fell back a step and took Sara with her.

The morning had turned muggy. A bead of sweat trickled down from Collin's temple. Another down his back, beneath his shirt.

As aware as he was of the weather, he was even more so that while Leo'd asked him to stand up and Evangeline had asked Alice, Coop was left out.

Their brother sat at the front of the crowd, Owen and August Mason on one side.

This morning, when Collin had pressed him, Coop had claimed he was happy for Collin to stand up for Leo.

Things had been strained between him and Leo these past weeks.

His expression as he sat with the watching crowd was inscrutable. Collin was reminded of that same tension that stretched between them the other night, when he'd asked his twin to swap shifts for the watch.

Coop was trying to turn over a new leaf. But could he

really do that if he kept up some of the behaviors that had sucked him into drinking in the first place?

Collin worried for his brother.

"We're gathered today to witness the marriage of these fine folks, Leo and Evangeline." Hollis's deep voice extended over the crowd.

He looked finer than Collin had ever seen him. The wagon master was usually dressed in trousers and a shirt, sometimes with a slicker over them to fend off the weather.

Today, he wore a clean, dark pair of trousers and a white shirt that would've passed for Sunday best back home. His dark brown skin was scrubbed clean from a recent washing.

He held a book open in his hands. When he spoke, it was with the same authority he used to command the entire wagon train of hundreds of people.

Collin had the urge to straighten up. This was serious business.

"Leo, will you take this woman to be your wife? To live together in holy matrimony?"

Collin wouldn't have said that his brother was an overly emotional sort of person. But Leo's voice was rough with emotion when he replied, "I will."

Hollis spoke again. "Evangeline, will you take this man to be your husband? To live together in holy matrimony?"

Standing beside Leo, Collin had a clear view of her face, the faint blush in her cheeks and the glint of tears in her eyes. "I will," she said.

"Repeat after me," Hollis went on.

Leo's voice was an echo a few seconds behind his, "I take you as my wedded wife... to have and to hold... from this day forward... for better, for worse... for richer and poorer... in sickness and health... to love and to cherish... till death do us part."

And then it was Evangeline's turn. Her voice began quiet, almost a whisper, but grew stronger with every phrase. "I take you as my wedded husband... to have and to hold... from this day forward... for better, for worse... for richer and poorer... in sickness and health... to honor and obey... till death do us part."

Leo gave a wet chuckle and raised one hand, still clasping Evangeline's to wipe a tear from his cheek. Standing close behind him, Collin hadn't seen it fall.

But he had a clear view of Coop's face, peaceful and glad. Coop was happy for Leo.

Collin felt a band of tension release somewhere in his chest.

Hollis announced the couple as man and wife for the first time and Leo kissed Evangeline, a chaste brush of his lips against hers.

The crowd around them cheered and whooped.

Leo was quick to scoop up Sara. He held her in one arm, his other arm around Evangeline's waist.

Collin patted his brother on the back. "Congratulations."

Leo didn't have time to answer as Alice hugged Evangeline and then they were set upon by well-wishers.

Owen, still the acting captain of their company, approached. Collin caught the tension around his eyes as he glanced at Evangeline and away. Collin had watched Owen try to befriend her, maybe try to win her hand in the early days of their journey. Even then, she'd only had eyes for Leo.

He detoured around the happy couple and moved toward Hollis.

Collin didn't pay much attention. Instead, he looked over the crowd for Stella.

"I don't like the feel of this weather," Hollis said to Owen. "It's too warm for this time of year. Could be a big storm brewing."

Collin caught sight of her, in his hat, head bent as she spoke with Maddie amongst the crowd now breaking up into smaller groups. There'd be a celebration for Leo and Evangeline. He'd been asked to play his fiddle to allow for some dancing later.

He broke away from the wedding party, unable to stay away from Stella. She'd been jumpy and on edge this morning. What did she think of the frontier wedding?

"Morning, Miss Maddie. Stephen." He didn't have a hat to tip, so he settled for a smile.

Maddie gave him a distracted smile. Stella glared at him.

All of a sudden, Maddie gripped Stella's wrist. She was staring at something over Collin's shoulder. He turned to look. There were people milling about everywhere inside the circle of wagons.

And then he noticed someone he'd never seen before, a man in a hat too fancy for the wilds out here, and a dark vest and trousers covered in dust from the trail.

Behind him, Stella and Maddie where whispering furiously.

When he turned around, with eyebrows raised, they quit. Stella'd told him they were running from something. Did this man have something to do with it?

"Stephen said you'd offered shooting lessons," Louis said.

Collin hadn't even realized that the youth was standing next to Stella. He'd been too focused on her.

"I want to learn how to shoot," Louis said.

Stella looked like she wanted to shoot *Collin*, staring daggers at him.

When he turned his gaze on the younger brother, he stopped short. Because beneath that hat wasn't a boy at all.

He should've expected it. If he'd spared half a second to think about it, he might've guessed.

Louis wasn't *Louis* at all.

And up close, knowing what he knew about Stella, it was impossible not to notice.

She—whatever her name was—was staring at him with a frank question in her face.

He swallowed his surprise, knowing that's what Stella would want.

"Yeah, I can teach you, kid."

"Now?"

Stella cut off her not-brother's query with a slashed hand through the air. "Collin is going to be celebrating with his family."

She wasn't getting rid of him that easily. Maybe she hadn't asked for help, but her sister had. That counted for something.

"How about after supper tonight?" he countered.

Stella sighed even as the girl dressed as a boy grinned at him.

FELICITY VACKER CROUCHED inside the wagon, awkwardly balanced on top of the supplies stored inside. She was scrubbing the wagon floor near the tailgate, where she had spilled part of the pot of oatmeal they'd eaten for breakfast.

"That mess will keep." Abigail appeared from around the side of the wagon.

Felicity scrubbed harder.

Abigail was Felicity's fellow traveler. They hadn't known each other before the start of this journey, and had been thrown into close quarters from day one.

Abigail was one month older than Felicity's twenty-two years. She had light brown skin and dark hair and eyes.

Somehow, being around the bubbly young woman made Felicity feel old beyond her years.

"Everyone is gathering over near the Masons' wagon. I saw fiddles." Abigail's excitement was palpable.

Felicity didn't stop cleaning. "If we leave the mess, we might get an infestation of flies. Or other unwanted critters."

Abigail shuddered. Two days ago, she'd had a mouse run across her boot while she'd been getting ready for the day. Felicity figured they were in the mouse's way. They were the ones camping in the wilderness. The mouse had every right to be there.

But Abigail had shrieked as if the mouse had been a venomous snake.

Now Abigail sighed. "Will it really make that much of a difference if you scrub out the wagon now or in an hour? After we've celebrated the happy couple?"

Felicity had attended the worship service and wedding, along with most of the other travelers from their company. She'd watched two people that she knew only in passing because they were part of the same company pledge their lives to each other. Looking at them, it was obvious to see they were in love.

But watching the short ceremony had also opened up a hollow pit inside Abigail's stomach.

She didn't want to go to the celebration and experience that feeling again.

And she didn't enjoy crowds.

"You should go," Felicity said. "Have fun."

"Would it be so bad if you had a little fun, too?" Abigail grumbled the words under her breath.

"After I finish this, I'm going to take our laundry down to the creek for washing. Then I'll check on the oxen and start preparations for supper."

Abigail sighed again. "You make me feel like an absolute sluggard. Today is supposed to be a rest day. Hollis said so."

Felicity shook her head. Hollis had called for a halt today from the endless slog of walking alongside the wagon wheels. But Felicity knew it was for catching up on the work waiting to be done.

She also knew that some people needed to feel a certain comfort about their choices. She didn't know Abigail well enough. Maybe she was one of those people. "You're not a sluggard. You should go and enjoy the dancing."

The sound of an instrument being tuned reached their ears over the other noises of camp.

Abigail glanced across the circle of wagons. "Are you certain?"

"Mm hmm."

Abigail slipped away and Felicity went back to her work. One little chunk of oatmeal had stuck itself to the wood of the wagon bed and wouldn't come off.

She put some force behind her scrubbing.

Felicity found solace in the unending work this journey across the plains demanded. Work she knew. It was familiar and comforting, not like the questions that plagued her. Had she made the right choice leaving Massachusetts?

Work was one of her earliest memories. She couldn't have been older than four when she'd picked up a towel from the basket her stepmother Celia had taken down from the clothesline and began to fold it.

Celia had absolutely beamed at her when she'd seen Felicity folding the clean laundry. At that time, Celia had two small babies of her own and while she'd never been cold toward Felicity, there was a noticeable difference in her demeanor when Felicity helped with chores. She was happy when Felicity helped.

Felicity's childhood had become consumed with more and more chores as she'd grown, and as a third little sister came along, and then a brother, and another.

Every once in awhile, she would catch a look from her father, like a shadow passing behind his eyes. But Papa was too busy—or too afraid to speak up against Celia's wishes—to grant Felicity the relief of an afternoon off.

Was it any wonder she'd left home at sixteen and gone to the city to find work?

She finished scrubbing away the oatmeal and picked up her bucket of soapy water to get down from the wagon. Thinking about Papa and Celia wasn't productive.

But her thoughts remained tangled or maybe her boot had gotten wet because she slipped on the wagon wheel spokes as she clambered out of the wagon.

She let go of the bucket and made a grab for the tail-gate. Missed.

But a strong hand suddenly clasped her elbow, steadying her.

The help came a moment too late. Cold, sudsy water spilled down the front of her dress. She gasped.

And then gaped as she registered just who had come to her rescue.

He was tall and handsome, with a square jaw and dark eyes. She'd seen him around camp, driving a team of oxen and a wagon. He had a brother, Owen, one of the captains of their company.

"All right, miss?"

Shyness stole over her at the rumble of his voice. Her muscles froze up and her tongue tied itself in a knot.

The silence seemed to stretch and stretch as he waited for her answer. His friendly gaze changed as his brows drew together.

Say something.

But when her mouth finally opened, it was only to hang their uselessly. No words escaped. Embarrassment scalded her cheeks.

He was staring now, his expression shifting to concern. "Miss?"

He let go of her arm and that seemed to unlock her muscles—all of them except her tongue. She picked up her sodden skirts and scurried around the wagon, out of his sight. All the way down to the creek, which was empty of other travelers now that the wedding celebration was starting.

Felicity was breathing hard enough to drown out the trickle of the shallow water passing over its rocky stream bed. She pressed her hands to her hot cheeks.

Why couldn't she be less awkward? More like Abigail, who would've laughed off the accident and introduced herself to their handsome neighbor. Abigail was never tongue-tied. And she certainly wasn't shy.

Felicity itched for something to do with her hands. If she worked hard enough, maybe she could forget the embarrassment she'd just caused herself.

But she'd forgotten to grab the bundle of soiled clothing

in her haste to escape the campsite. Now she had to go all the way back to retrieve it.

Not yet. What if he was still nearby?

After the way she'd humiliated herself, the last thing she wanted to do was see him again.

SIX

Collin didn't like this.

August was helping Collin push the cattle. Nearby, the wagon train was all out of sorts. Usually, the wagons maintained a cohesive line.

Now some raced ahead. Others lagged behind, leaving gaps. Some men drove recklessly.

An hour ago, Hollis had interrupted the dancing and talking from Evangeline and Leo's wedding to ask them all to pack up as quickly as possible and move the wagons.

Many in the crowd had complained.

"Do you want to die? Because you will, if you stay out here."

Collin hadn't thought the threat was real, that Hollis was exaggerating.

But as the afternoon wore on, an eerie stillness had overtaken the wide-open prairie. A huge wall of clouds had built on the horizon and crept closer. The air seemed to grow heavier with each passing second.

Families had run to pack up their wagons, even left some things behind in the rush to get somewhere safe.

But how was moving any safer than the ring of wagons had been?

On horseback, Hollis guided the wagons toward a vast dip in the flat landscape.

But where were they supposed to put the herd of cattle? The animals didn't like the building storm any more than Collin did.

Lightning struck on the horizon, and thunder rumbled so loudly it seemed to shake the ground.

Collin pushed the cattle even harder, though he couldn't guess how this lower ground was going to afford them any real protection.

The sky changed from slate gray to an ominous tinge of green.

The cattle seemed to react to something in the air. They bawled and kicked, trying to move faster.

August shouted something, but he was on the opposite side of the herd. Collin couldn't make out his words, but he was waving toward the wagon train.

Collin squinted, trying to see any of his family in the jumble of wagons. Someone's canvas covering had come loose and was waving wildly. He knew Leo and Coop would be doing their best to protect Alice and Evangeline and Sara.

The clouds churned overhead as wind snatched at Collin's clothing and blew dust into his face. He pulled up the kerchief around his neck to cover his nose and mouth. His hat would've been useful right about now, but Stella still had it.

Stella.

He scanned the nearest wagons, hoping for a glimpse of

her black beast. The stallion was racing between wagons, Stella clinging to its back.

Was the horse out of control? He couldn't tell whether Stella was guiding it at such a wild speed or not.

August's voice rose above the roaring of the wind. Collin glanced back toward him to see the cattle scattering.

But Stella might need help—

There was no time to weigh his options. He went with his gut and abandoned the cattle, wheeled his horse and rode toward the wagon train and Stella.

She must have been guiding the stallion, because her animal turned toward Collin.

They were still twenty yards apart when another terrific roll of thunder came. No—not thunder. The sound didn't abate.

A terrible roar, like a steam locomotive bearing down on them, made Collin look up.

A funnel dropped from the churning clouds and dust rose from the ground where it landed.

Tornado!

He meant to shout a warning, but the wind snatched his voice the moment he opened his mouth.

Stella looked over her shoulder. He saw her terror in the way she kicked the horse.

The tornado was barreling across the prairie, ripping trees and shrubs and tossing them into the air as if they were sawdust. It was headed straight toward the wagon train spread across the plain.

As Collin watched, a wagon at the front of the snaking line was tossed on its side as if it was a child's plaything.

Breath hitched in his chest. He didn't know who was inside that wagon and could only pray they'd jumped clear before it had toppled.

He'd drawn closer to Stella now. Her hat was askew and when she looked at him, her eyes were wild.

"What's the matter?" he shouted.

"Our wagon—axle busted. My sisters—!"

That's why she'd been riding as if the devil himself was on her tail. Their wagon had broken down. In this terrible storm, likely no one had stopped to assist them.

There was no helping the wagons in front of them. Unless the twister changed its path, there was nothing Collin could do. He'd be sucked up into the funnel cloud if he got too close.

But maybe he could help Stella's sisters get to safety.

He sent one last glance toward the cattle, now scattered across the prairie, running for their lives. August was nowhere to be seen.

He took off after Stella. He thought he saw her brush at her face with one gloved hand. Was she crying? He didn't have time to process the emotion of the loss he'd just witnessed.

The roaring around them grew louder. Collin pushed his gelding closer to her stallion. They raced past wagons scattering every direction, fearful travelers trying to get out of the path of the tornado's destruction.

It was no use.

Collin glanced over his shoulder and found the tornado bearing down. He veered his horse to the right, almost running into Stella's stallion.

"We have to get out of the way!" he called out.

"My sisters are up ahead!"

He could only pray that they'd abandoned the wagon and run.

"There's no time!" He could feel the threat in the air

now, the tornado trying to pull him from his horse. They needed to cut away, go south.

"You go, then!" she cried.

He wasn't going to let her get killed.

He edged even closer to her horse—close enough to quickly wrap his arm around her waist.

She shrieked as he pulled her free of the stallion's saddle.

He barely kept his seat as she fought against him. He wheeled his horse, kicking it into the fastest gallop the gelding could give.

Stella beat against him with her fists, twisting and writhing. She caught him in the jaw and his head snapped to the side.

But he didn't let her go. And his gelding held true, probably as frightened by the storm as Collin was. The stallion raced along beside them.

"Let go of me!" Stella screamed.

The bite of the wind lessened the slightest amount, but he didn't dare turn back to look lest he lose his precarious hold on Stella.

"My sisters!" she screamed in his ear.

He understood her fear. He didn't know where Leo or Alice or Coop were. What if they were injured? What if the tornado had sucked them up into the sky?

But killing himself wasn't going to help them now, and his strength was no match for Mother Nature's.

"It's going to turn," he told her. It had to. It had to.

Please turn.

Stinging rain and tiny hail began to pelt them, quickly soaking through their clothes.

Stella's struggles had lessened now, and she sank against him, her fingers clutching his shoulder like claws.

She was strong, but she was so small that his size and strength dwarfed hers.

And then the roar abated. He finally glanced back to see the tornado's funnel disappear up into the clouds where it had come from.

STELLA COULDN'T STOP SHAKING.

Collin held her against him, and she'd momentarily lost the strength to fight him.

She couldn't get her mind's eye to stop replaying what she'd just seen. Over Collin's shoulder, she'd had an unimpeded view of the tornado as it had wreaked havoc on the wagon train. Wagons thrown aside as if the conveyances with two thousand pounds of supplies weighed nothing. One wagon had been smashed to smithereens, pieces no bigger than matchsticks as she'd watched. She could only pray whoever had been in that wagon had run away before it had happened.

She had been directly in the path of the tornado, stubbornly riding toward her sisters, before Collin had pulled her off the horse. She could've died.

Maddie. Lily.

She tried to stop her thoughts from replaying those terrifying moments. It was worse when she closed her eyes and then opened them with a gasp against Collin's shoulder.

When one of their wagon's wheels had broken, she'd had only one thought: find Collin. Collin would help them. She'd jumped on the back of her stallion and ridden away, leaving Maddie and Lily and Irene behind, not knowing what was coming.

Where were her sisters? Had they survived? Maybe the tornado had lifted before it had reached the Fairfax wagon.

"I'm going to lower you down," Collin said. His voice was rough. He'd been looking at the devastation left behind, too. The band of his arm loosened around her. He bent in the saddle until her feet touched the ground.

She grabbed onto the back of his saddle for a few moments, until her unsteady knees decided to hold her.

The rain worsened, beating against her.

Collin made a clucking sound. He was calling to the stallion, she realized.

"We've got to get back," he said. "Folks will need help. Some might be injured." Or dead. He didn't say that aloud, but he had to be thinking it, just like she was.

A stand of taller grass waved just in front of them.

Then two things happened at the same time.

The pressure in the air changed as the sky began to roar again. Louder this time.

And a flock of dozens of blackbirds flew up and out of the long grasses, startling Collin's horse.

The horse reared and whinnied.

Wind blew so hard against Stella's back that she stumbled and almost went to her knees.

Collin lost his seat on the horse.

Before she could so much as move a muscle, both horses had bolted.

Collin struggled against the wind to regain his feet. When he looked in her direction, she saw pure terror on his face.

Her hat flew off her head. She glanced over her shoulder. Another tornado extended down from the sky. Much closer this time.

She didn't know if she screamed. Maybe Collin shouted her name.

She couldn't hear over the roar of noise and wind.

His big hand grabbed her arm.

Something large—a tree root? A panel from a wagon?—flew through the air, missing them by only a few feet. If something like that hit them—

Collin must've had the same thought, because he pulled her to the ground.

Fear choked her as Collin pushed her face-down into the ground, lying with his chest and shoulders atop her midsection. He blocked both of their heads with his arms.

The obliterating roar of the tornado grew louder, until it was all she could hear.

Wind sucked at her clothes, lifted one of her legs from the ground.

She screamed, but she couldn't even hear her own voice.

Collin pressed harder against her, pressed her into the ground.

Against her back, she could feel his heartbeat pounding through the thin layers of clothes between them.

It became the only thing she could focus on.

Ka-thump. Ka-thump.

They were going to die out here.

Ka-thump. Ka-thump.

It was her fault. She'd brought her sisters here.

Ka-thump. Ka-thump.

Was it all for nothing then? All the scrapping?

Ka-thump. Ka-thump.

All the hours working under her horrible seamstress boss? Working until her fingers were cracked and bleeding from cold?

Ka-thump. Ka-thump.

She'd never fallen in love. She'd thought she had time.

Ka-thump. Ka-thump.

She'd cared more for her sisters than her own happiness.

Ka-thump. Ka-thump.

She'd killed them all.

Ka-thump. Ka-thump.

Ka-thump. Ka-thump.

Ka-thump. Ka-thump.

Collin's fingers threaded through her hair, torn loose from its confinement by the wind. Then she realized that the roaring of the storm was lifting, that it was moving off.

"Hey," his voice came from too close, his jaw moved against her temple when he spoke. "We're alive. We're all right."

She wasn't all right.

She was crying, great heaving sobs that he wouldn't mistake because of the way they were pressed together.

She rocked her shoulders and he moved off of her as eerie silence descended upon them.

She scrambled to a sitting position, put a few feet between them.

His arms were half-outstretched, as if he wanted to reach for her. After a moment of her staring at him, he dropped them. Then patted his chest. He seemed a little frantic as he reached in the collar of his shirt and pulled out something on a string. She saw a metallic flash.

He sighed in relief. "My mother's," he murmured as he tucked the cord back under his shirt.

She gulped, trying to stem the tears that helped absolutely no one.

Even the rain had slowed to only a slow, gentle patter.

Miles away, behind the storm, golden rays of sunlight arced toward the ground. It seemed wrong to see such a beautiful sight in the wake of such destruction.

"All right?" Collin asked.

She shook her head. "My sisters," she said in a tear-choked voice.

"We'll find them. They'll be okay."

"You can't know that!" Her voice rose and she angrily wiped at the moisture on her cheeks. It didn't help. Her hands were soaked and dirty.

How could this man see the devastation around them and believe that her sisters were all right? Did he only ever see the bright side of things?

He didn't seem perturbed that she'd shouted at him.

He stood up, brushed himself off, pulled his wet shirt away from his skin.

He extended a hand to her. She let him help her up. This close, she could see a rivulet of blood where his jaw and ear met.

"Are you hurt?" she demanded.

Something flickered in his eyes. Then his brows crunched in a question.

She lifted on tiptoe to touch just beneath his jaw, get a closer look. Her breath caught at the nearness, her emotions still swinging wildly. She couldn't quite believe they were alive.

"You've got a nasty scrape," she murmured, stepping back.

"It'll keep." He whistled. Then whistled again.

Waited.

And there came his horse, trotting toward him, reins loose and dragging the ground.

To her complete shock, the stallion followed.

Collin waited until the gelding came right up to him, whickering.

"What a good old boy you are," Collin said. There was clear affection in his voice.

The stallion stopped a few feet behind Collin's gelding. She slowly approached. Miraculously, the stallion stayed where he was.

Collin was running his hands over the gelding's neck and shoulder. "You'll want to look him over, make sure he hasn't been injured."

The horses were slick with rain, skin quivering with latent fear, but unscathed.

"We've got to get back to the wagons," Collin said finally, though only a few minutes must've passed.

"I have to find my sisters."

But before either of them had swung into the saddle, she panicked.

"My hair!" She patted the wet mass tumbled around her shoulders. Her hat—Collin's hat—was completely gone.

It was ridiculous in the wake of such a terrible tragedy, but she was shaking all over at the thought of being found out.

"I've got an idea." Collin was unruffled, as always. He rifled through his saddlebag. "I've got an extra shirt..."

He pulled a blue shirt from his saddlebag and began ripping it into strips as he walked toward her.

"Pull your hair up," he said.

She didn't know what he meant, but she squeezed some of the water out of her hair and began to twirl it into a knot.

"We'll pretend you've got a head injury," he said quietly, lifting one of the strips of fabric to wind around her head. "Until we can find you a hat."

The man confounded her.

She hadn't been very kind to him, but he still protected her. She'd felt such a strong beat of relief when she'd seen him ride toward her.

It was dangerous to rely on him. She knew it.

But for now, she didn't have a choice.

SEVEN

Felicity came to with a terrible pounding in her head. What had happened?

Her memory was as fuzzy as a ball of woolen yarn.

She and Abigail had been in a hurry...

The wind...

A terrible noise...

And then darkness.

Why couldn't she remember?

Abigail.

She tried to say her friend's name, but the attempt caused an awful pain in her throat, as if her vocal cords had been severed with a knife. She tried to reach up but she couldn't move her arms.

Tears rolled from the corners of her eyes, down her temples and into her hair. She was already wet, she realized. Rain was splattering on her face and hair and the rest of her.

Had her eyes closed?

She opened them to see a gray, cloudy sky and more rain. a tall tree in her line of sight sat at an angle that made her dizzy, its branches hanging over her.

She tried to move, but a great weight covered her body. What—?

She craned her neck, the movement sending railroad spikes of pain through her skull.

She was half-buried underneath a mass of splintered wood and tattered canvas. Their wagon. Hers and Abigail's.

She recognized the gingham dress sticking out among the mess. Her own Sunday dress that had been stowed in the wagon. She also spied a book with a blue cover that belonged to Abigail.

Where was Abigail?

Felicity tried calling out, fear for her friend rising in her breast. She only made a whisper of sound and it cost her dearly, such pain as she'd never known.

What had happened to the wagon train? She was shaking and terrified, trapped and injured.

Had anyone survived?

She strained her ears but heard nothing other than the pitter-patter of rain and far-off clap of thunder.

If she couldn't get herself free, she would die out here. She could feel the weakness creeping through her limbs. Warm liquid pooled on her sternum and then dripped down her neck. Was she bleeding?

She had come on this journey to find a life she would never have back home. She'd wanted more than working over a sewing form day after day, until her fingers cramped and her eyes blurred and her back ached.

But not this...

She didn't want to die out here. Maybe no one would even find her body.

She tried to grasp control of her spinning thoughts. Told herself there was no use sinking into worry.

But she couldn't help it.

Maybe if she could free one hand...

She wiggled her right hand, then her left. Moving her left hand caused a deep throb of pain and she instantly stopped.

She heard a shout. Who—?

She heard sounds of wet fabric rubbing together, then footsteps.

A shadow passed over her face.

She blinked up and realized her eyes had closed again. How much time had passed?

A familiar face bent over her.

Not Abigail.

She recognized the same man who'd helped her near her wagon.

"Hullo, there," he said.

She might've been embarrassed if she wasn't in so much pain. She tried to speak, and would've cried out at the pain if she'd had any voice. What was wrong with her voice?

His eyes flickered over her before his big hand produced a handkerchief and pressed it to her neck.

"Did that hurt, when you tried to speak?" He quickly corrected himself. "Just blink. Twice for yes, once for no."

She blinked twice.

"All right. I'm going to help you. I'm August Mason."

August. She already knew his name.

The rain had stopped, leaving the air feeling muggy. Or maybe that was her face, heating because of his nearness.

And a spot of her embarrassment.

A female voice called out, and August raised his head. "She's here!"

Who—?

Abigail. Felicity registered running footsteps. Within moments, Abigail knelt by her head, opposite August.

Abigail's expression told her far more than August's had. Her brown eyes were dark and frightened, the medium brown of her skin pulled tight over her face with worry. "Oh, no!"

"It hurts her to speak," August cautioned.

Felicity blinked twice. *Yes.*

Abigail was usually neat in her appearance, but now her hair had come loose from the bun she'd worn earlier and her dress was smudged with dirt.

Was that how Felicity looked, too? Even worse, did she have blood all over her?

"We need to get her out from underneath this debris," August said. "Can you hold this? We've got to stop the bleeding."

Abigail shifted around Felicity's head. The movement loosened something. Felicity had thought she was lying on the ground. She hadn't known there was wreckage from the wagon beneath her until it dug painfully into her lower back.

She couldn't cry out, but she must've made some indication of pain because August bodily moved Abigail to his side. "Better?"

The pain had eased off as Abigail's weight was lifted and moved.

Two blinks. *Yes.*

August showed Abigail how to hold the handkerchief the way he was. "I don't know how deep this cut is. She may need stitches. I'm worried she's injured somewhere else we can't see."

Was she? The pain in her left arm had grown, now a constant throbbing. She was so weighted down that she couldn't tell what hurt—everything hurt. She would be a mess of bruises in the morning.

"I'm going to be as careful as I can."

Oh. He was speaking to her.

Felicity focused on his face in the growing dusk.

"If I do something that hurts ya, I want you to blink a bunch of times in a row. Can you do that for me, lass?"

"Her name is Felicity," Abigail said.

"Felicity. Nice to meet you." His warm, soft look made her stomach do a slow flip.

She'd re-imagined that first meeting between them as she'd washed laundry at the creek. Imagined herself *not* falling out of the wagon. Not with a drenched dress. In her imagination, she'd introduced herself with a calm charm she would never affect in real life.

Her imagined introduction hadn't been like this. With her weak, helpless, voiceless.

"Let's get you out of here," he said.

Two blinks. *Yes.*

He was careful where he stepped.

He moved big boards and—was that the axle? A metal-and-wood wheel was lugged aside. Oh, was he strong.

She couldn't seem to look away as he dragged pieces of the wagon off of her. So much wreckage.

"We'll have you out of here in no time," Abigail said softly. She pushed Felicity's sodden hair back from her forehead.

Felicity had never seen her friend so worried. Abigail was typically a ray of sunshine, chattering about this or that, or singing. She had a beautiful singing voice. She was Felicity's opposite in almost every way. Felicity was shy. Abigail was outgoing. Felicity was tall and slender. Abigail was a few inches shorter and curved in all the right places.

Of the two of them, Felicity was the worrier. Abigail always the optimist.

Felicity must look especially bad.

When August hefted a heavy barrel Felicity felt the first of the weight lift away.

The release of the weight and pressure enabled her to take the first deep breath in a long time.

Her right arm came loose of the debris.

And a cascade of pain ran down the left side of her midsection.

COLLIN KEPT EVEN with Stella as they rode toward the broken line of wagons.

The sun was slipping toward the horizon at too fast a clip. There had to be folks injured. Maybe lost, if they'd run away from the twister.

How were they going to find everybody in the dark?

He knew Stella was anxious to locate her sisters. He'd had a close look at her show of emotion, her tears.

Even so, when they came even with a wagon turned on its side, the side panel splintered in two and no oxen in sight, Stella slowed her horse.

"Anyone there?" she called out. "Do you need help?"

A shadow moved from behind the tipped wagon. A woman stood up.

Collin didn't miss the revolver she held in one shaking hand.

She wasn't pointing it at them, but he put out his hand anyway, to caution Stella.

"We ain't hurt," the woman said. She was bedraggled, and a scratch on one side of her face belied her statement.

For the first time, Collin noticed two small children huddling at her side.

"My man went to find help. See if someone can help us right our wagon."

Stella nodded. "We're looking for my—for my family," she fumbled her words, glanced sideways at him as if it was his fault. She firmed her chin and spoke to the woman once more. "We got separated. After—after we find them, we'll come back."

A look of relief passed over the woman's face. She nodded.

Stella kept riding. Collin did too.

"That was a whole lot of *we's* back there," he murmured when they'd put some distance between them and the wagon.

She glanced at him, and that silly bandage around her head made him want to smile. It was a little ridiculous how many times they'd had to wrap his torn shirt around her head to hide her hair. He could only hope it would hold and that everyone would be too concerned with themselves to look too closely at her.

"If you need to find your family, you should go." She kept her gaze forward.

"You're not rid of me yet," he said. "It's all right to lean on me a little—"

Her soft gasp cut off his words.

They'd been loosely following a trail of debris, tree branches and bits of wood and canvas and other things littering the prairie.

Ahead was a wagon that had been destroyed. He urged the gelding to a faster clip but then reined in a bit away. He didn't want to risk the gelding stepping on something sharp and becoming lame.

"Anyone there?" he called out.

Stella reined in behind him.

When he got off his horse, she stayed mounted.

"Collin."

He took a few steps toward the wreck, waiting for her to call him back.

"Be careful," she cautioned.

"I will." A few more steps and he was on top of the broken wagon. It was in pieces, the canvas ripped and torn.

"Anybody need help?" he asked.

A soft groan answered him.

"There's someone here," he called over his shoulder to Stella.

"I'm coming." He barely registered the sounds of her sliding out of the saddle and approaching.

There was so much destruction. Wood, pieces of barrels, food, clothes. He was afraid to step on any of it. Afraid someone might be buried beneath.

"Where are you?" he called out. "How many of you are there?"

"I'm over here." There it was. A male voice, coming from a few feet to his right. There was a rustling. Was that a hand waving?

"My leg's trapped," the voice said. "Do you see my wife?"

Stella had been moving toward Collin, who was trying to pick his way carefully through the debris. Now she stopped and scanned the area around her.

"I'm coming to free you," Collin told the man. "What's your wife's name?"

"Elinor." Another groan. "Can you—can you hurry?"

Collin stumbled when one of the boards he'd stepped on shifted beneath him.

Stella was ranging farther away from where he was, calling out Elinor's name.

Collin knew she was anxious to find her sisters, but her compassionate heart had bade her stop and help this couple who needed it.

He liked her. Fiery spirit, protective nature. He knew she had secrets, and they only made him want to know her more.

Collin finally got close enough to see the man's arm and shoulder buried beneath several large pieces of wagon bed.

"You see my oxen?" the man asked.

Collin glanced around, his eyes landing on the two oxen, still in their yoke. Unmoving.

"I think their necks might be broken," he said as he knelt to start freeing the man.

Dark, glittering eyes assessed him as he started pulling boards away. There's where the man was stuck. The heavy wagon bed had landed on top of his lower body.

"You in pain?" Collin asked.

"Some. Just git me outta here."

As the darkness began to roll in, moving the wrecked wagon unlocked something inside Collin. A memory of that night, months ago, that had changed everything.

He could almost taste the choking smoke, feel the fear and confusion in the air.

He tried to shake away the memories from that night at the powder mill, but they clung to him as he finally got close enough to the wagon bed to free the man.

Collin braced his legs and was able to lift it a few inches, long enough for the man to pull himself out from underneath.

"Collin!" Stella's voice rang out as he offered his hand to the man whose name he didn't even know.

The man was a little wobbly on his feet and covered in scratches and dirt but otherwise seemed all right.

Seeing his face recalled a visceral memory of Rolf's soot-stained face.

"Collin!" Stella yelled again, and he was shaken out of the memory.

He hurried to where Stella knelt on the ground next to a prone body.

"She's unconscious," Stella said. "I can't tell if she's hurt. I don't want to move her."

Collin leaned close and felt the puff of the woman's breath against his cheek. "She's alive, at least."

The husband had come up behind them, then moved around to kneel at his wife's side. "Elinor. Can you hear me?"

The last of the sun's rays disappeared over the horizon.

Stella gripped Collin's wrist. He knew she had to be thinking about her sisters. Now they were out there somewhere in the dark.

"We need to make a couple of torches," he said.

He stood up and moved away a couple of feet, bending over a ripped piece of canvas from the remains of the wagon. "You mind if we rip this up—?"

The sound of a hammer being cocked drew him up short.

The man he'd helped had stood up, drawn his gun, and was holding it on Collin.

"That's our property," he growled. "Don't take what ain't yours."

Collin wanted to argue that the canvas was so torn that it wouldn't be useful any more. It would need to be replaced.

But it was obvious the man meant business. One squeeze of his finger on the trigger and Collin might be dead.

"All right." He tried to make his voice sound easygoing, but it was difficult. "We helped you get free, now you can take care of your Elinor. We've gotta ride on and find our families."

He motioned Stella away and was relieved when she followed. She must've been as shaken as he was by that turn of events.

Collin didn't want to think it, but they needed to get out of here before the man did something else—like try to steal their horses.

He backed away. He wanted to take Stella's arm, but that might look funny. She was supposed to be a man, supposed to be able to handle herself.

"Get on your horse," he said, voice low.

For once, she didn't argue.

They both mounted up and wasted no time riding away.

EIGHT

They had ridden away from that last couple quickly, Stella's fear spiking. They hadn't had to go far to find material to make a torch. There were scattered pieces of wood and fabric, some of it the shape of dresses and pants. all over the prairie.

Collin had worked with meticulous quickness, winding strips of fabric around a long piece of wood and then using his flint and tinder from his saddlebag to light it.

She had been glad to have him with her.

They didn't run across any other folks needing help before they reached the Fairfax family wagon, thankfully far behind where the twister had hit the other wagons. No one else had stopped to help her family. No one but Collin.

Stella jumped from her horse, her sisters' names on her lips, but it was clear from the moment her boots touched the ground that they weren't here.

The wagon was still intact, though the wheel that had broken made the wagon list to one side. There was no movement other than the oxen, still waiting in their traces. A tail swished.

One corner of the wagon covering flapped loose in the wind. She lost the last bit of hope when she pulled open the canvas.

No one was inside.

Her heart beat so strongly in her ears that she barely heard Collin's voice. "Look here."

He had come down from his horse and was waving the torch over an area outside around the wagon. "There's a man's boot print here. I'm guessing your sister doesn't wear a size this big."

She moved to crouch near his feet, reaching out to touch the imprint in a spot of mud. The boot size was far too large for Lily's foot. She swallowed hard. "You're right."

"There're more prints here." He moved the torch to his other side, where a horse's hoofprints were clearly visible. "Maybe someone came to help them."

Maybe someone had come to *find them*.

"How long ago do you think these prints were made?" She glanced up into his face in the flickering torch light and saw his thoughtful expression.

"It would've been after the rain passed over," he said. "Or the rain would've washed the prints away."

Fear lodged in her throat.

"Maybe they left before he got here."

She had told her sisters to stay with the wagon, but if they'd seen the approaching storm in time, they would have run for cover. Wouldn't they?

She spun on her heel, turning a circle, trying to remember the landscape. In the dark, she couldn't see past the circle of light thrown by Collin's torch.

Had there been a snaking line of trees off to the south? Maybe they'd hoped to find cover there.

"I don't see any tracks leading away." He rounded the entire wagon. "But I guess it's possible they left before the storm hit."

Her heart was in her throat. She couldn't afford to break down, but the same emotions that had boiled over earlier choked her with tears now.

"Let's ground tie the oxen," he said. "It's gonna take some fixing to get your wagon rolling again. They can graze tonight and hopefully we can find someone to help us tomorrow."

She felt an echo of the same terror she had felt in New York. The fear of someone chasing them who intended to do them harm.

"Is that necessary? Can't we just go?"

He had already moved toward the oxen yoke but now stopped and looked at her, that torch still in his hand.

"It'll be all right. We know they were here. Hopefully they left the wagon to take shelter somewhere."

Hysteria rose inside her.

He must have seen it, because he planted the torch in the ground and came to her. "What if he found them?"

"He?" she echoed.

He saw too much. He always did. Now his eyes glittered, expression hard and not open like it'd been before. "Do you want to tell me who you're running from?"

She shook her head, unable to find words.

"I've let you keep your secrets up till now. But I'm not aiming to get myself killed. I need to know what I'm walking into."

He was right.

"Why have you been helping me?"

"The Good Book says we should help our neighbors. I figure if you're running from something, there's a reason for it."

He stepped closer to her. When had he gotten so close? She hadn't realized that he was only an arms' length away.

He reached out and brushed her cheek with his thumb. The touch was tender and unexpected. His hand fell away even as her chest expanded.

She didn't know if it was her rising emotion or his demand, but the words started to spill from her.

"There was nothing left for us in Dublin. My sisters and I had been saving up for years. A friend of a friend had an aunt who had come to America and written letters back. She said there was opportunity here. A better life. We paid our fares to cross the ocean and within days of stepping foot on American soil, all of our belongings were stolen. All of our money. We were left with nothing."

She saw the crease of his frown on his strong brow. She sniffled and straightened her shoulders. "There was an Irish lad who worked at the boarding house where we were staying and when he heard about our plight, he told us he knew someone who could help us."

Collin's frown was dark now, his face an echo of the thunder clouds that had caused such a storm earlier.

"Did they hurt you? Whoever it was who was supposed to help you?"

She shook her head. "They didn't have a chance. They put us up in a horrible tenement apartment. One tiny room for all three of us. They found us work in the factory, but it was—it was worse than back home. Our wages were so low. There was no hope of saving up enough to get out. And then one night, as we were walking home, a man dressed in a fancy suit came and walked beside us. He knew about us somehow, knew our situation. He focused on Maddie. Told her that she could earn a lot more than the pittance she was earning in the factory if she came to work for him."

Stella shuddered thinking about it. Naïve, hopeful Maddie had lit up, but Stella's stomach had been knotted with dread. Why would he want to help them? What was in it for him?

"We stayed up all night whispering about it. I knew it wasn't real, his offer. It was just another way to trap us."

He moved off toward the oxen, taking off the yoke so he could tie them off, just like he'd said.

She kept talking. "I couldn't talk her out of meeting with him. I followed her, and once she'd gone inside what looked like an apartment building, I tried to sneak inside too. That's where I met Irene."

He glanced over his shoulder. "She's not your aunt?"

She shook her head tightly. She was trusting him with a lot.

"Irene told me later that she took one look at me and knew I was going to cause trouble. She was tired of the life she had there. She'd been used up, moved into a different role. She said she didn't want to see another innocent girl be broken by that life."

But Stella had a suspicion that Irene had other motives for helping them. She had wanted out. But was that all?

"She knew where the brothers who ran everything on that side of town kept one of their safes, in an office. We stole back the money that had been taken from us and we ran."

His brow wrinkled. "And?"

She shook her head in confusion. What did he mean?

"How'd they know it was you?"

She'd never thought about that. Irene had told her no

one would be in the building that night. Had someone seen them?

"Irene was frightened from the moment we left. There were men who followed us at the train station. We barely got away from them. Irene swears she saw them again in Independence, but we slipped away."

"How much did you steal?"

"Not more than had been taken from us. I can't prove it —but everything happened so neatly, once our money had been stolen. The apartment, the factory jobs. And we had only settled in long enough to be miserable before one of the Byrne brothers came with this offer."

"You think they stole your money in the first place."

She shrugged. "It doesn't matter now. I need to keep my sisters safe. I want the new life we came to America for." The fierceness in her voice shook her.

She didn't know whether she expected him to believe her, or to walk away. He could tell Hollis that she had been lying this whole time. Maybe even get her kicked out of the wagon train. She had given him her secrets.

The question was, what would he do with them?

THEY HADN'T FOUND Stella's sisters by the time the torch sputtered out and the half-moon rose.

As the hours went on and night turned into early morn-ing, Collin grew more and more tired. He knew Stella had to be feeling the same.

They'd ridden south, to a line of trees that snaked along the landscape next to a creek. If Irene and Stella's sisters wanted to stay out of sight, the cover the trees would give them made sense.

But they'd been riding along the tree line for hours. First, they'd gone west.

They had turned around when there had been no sign of anyone after nearly two hours.

Now they backtracked the way they had come and traveled at least another mile past that.

Had Stella's sisters gotten turned around? They were city girls, so maybe they didn't know that you were supposed to stay still if you got lost.

His entire body was sinking with exhaustion and when he glanced over at Stella, he caught her as she nodded off and then came to with a jerk. Her stallion must've objected to the quick movement, because it whickered softly.

"I know you're desperate to find your sisters, but we need to catch a couple hours of shut-eye. Neither of us are at our best, and we're likely to miss some sign of them being this sleepy."

He saw from the slight way her lips opened that she wanted to argue with him. He admired her stubborn nature, that she wanted to do anything that she could to get to her sisters. He felt the same way about Leo and Alice and Coop.

But neither of them were going to be any good if they kept drifting off on the back of their horses.

"The horses need to rest too," he said quietly.

She acquiesced with a sigh.

"Only a couple of hours," she agreed as she reined in the stallion.

He found a little spot a few yards back from the banks of the shallow creek. Some time ago, an old grandfather of a tree had fallen pulling some of its roots out of the earth with it. Now it formed a natural barrier. One that would keep them from the stiff breeze that had blown in during the night.

Neither of them had their bedrolls, so they would have to make do with their saddle blankets. At this time of year, there was still a bite in the air.

He ground tied his horse and made sure that the stallion was safely tied off as Stella dragged her heavy saddle over.

When he carried his saddle and blanket toward her, the place he had that seemed plenty big all of a sudden looked much smaller.

He wouldn't have balked at sharing the small space with Coop or Leo or even Alice. But thinking about sharing the space with Stella made everything feel different.

He hadn't meant to reach out and touch her earlier. He'd done some courting back home in New Jersey, though there had never been anyone that he had given a serious thought to marrying. He couldn't say why he had reached out to touch Stella in that moment, only that it had felt necessary.

She was already lying down and didn't seem to notice his awkwardness.

"I'll put myself here," he said. He used his saddle for a pillow, just like he had so many nights on the trail. The saddle blanket only covered his upper body but that was all right.

Stella wriggled beside him, only inches away.

He was aware of her every movement. The way she shifted onto her back, then her shoulder, so she faced him. The soft sound of her breathing.

He'd thought he was sleepy enough to drift right off, but that wasn't true. Not with her this close. Not with him wanting her closer.

She moved again, tipping her head to the side.

Go to sleep, he willed her.

But she sighed. "I can't seem to calm my mind."

He stretched the fingers of one hand wide and then made a loose fist. "Maybe you should talk a little, then."

She hummed softly. "I've talked too much tonight." A pause. "Tell me about your family?"

"It's been the four of us for years," he said. "My father passed when Coop and I were little tykes." He bent one arm and rested his head on it, staring up at the star-littered sky. "Leo left his schooling and started working at the powder mill. I reckon he was... nine or ten?"

"So young?" She barely breathed the words and when he turned his head to look at her, he expected her to be drifting off.

She wasn't. Her gaze was on him, though he couldn't read her eyes in the dark.

"How old were you?" he asked. "When you went to work in that factory?"

"Sixteen."

He wanted to ask her more about it; wanted to know what she'd felt, if she'd been frightened, if she'd been resentful.

But he kept talking. "Leo was fifteen when our ma died and he took charge of all of us. A lot of responsibility fell on his shoulders, and he stepped up to it."

"You're close to him," she said.

"He's a good man."

"And your younger brother?"

Collin stared up at the sky again because it was easier than meeting her curious gaze. "He's a good man, too. Underneath. He's been through... some rough times."

He still believed it. He had to. Even with the memory

of that night back home, of smoke in his eyes and choking his breath.

Coop was better than how he'd acted on the first part of the journey.

"I remember this one time..." He let an affectionate smile creep onto his face. "We must've been about eight and every day when we walked to school we passed this house where an older couple lived. She baked all kinds of things that always smelled so good... The day before our birthday when we passed by her house, we smelled apple pie—Coop's favorite. He darted off the street before I could even blink and came back with that pie in his hands—raced off before I could catch him."

He snorted. "It was a stupid thing to do. But money was tight and he wanted a birthday treat. Our teacher found out about it and handed out a whipping—only I took it for him. I didn't want him to have to take it on his birthday."

He hadn't thought about that day in a long time. Years, probably. What had brought it to mind tonight?

"But if you took the punishment for him, that meant you got whipped on your birthday."

His smile faded a little. Maybe the story hadn't painted his brother in the best light.

"We were both missing our pa. Ma worked a lot; Leo did too. Maybe Coop deserved that whipping, but..."

"You've got a compassionate heart," she said when his voice trailed off.

Maybe he liked the admiration in her voice a little too much.

She shivered, and he turned his head toward her again. "You cold?"

"A little. Do you think we could...?" She scooted slightly closer.

He edged over until their shoulders were touching. He didn't know about her, but he was warmer just from the small contact.

They didn't speak again. He watched the stars until her head lolled against his shoulder.

His heart thumped in his ears, drowning out all of the night sounds around him.

When he tipped his head slightly, his jaw brushed her temple.

She acted tough. Took care of her sisters and did what needed to be done.

But in this moment, she seemed vulnerable.

And he liked being the one she leaned on. Even if she could only truly lean on him when she was unconscious.

NINE

Stella woke with a crick in her neck and no sense of where she was.

The first rays of sunlight were breaking through the darkness and she could make out the outlines of trees and branches overhead.

The woods.

A soft burbling had her remembering the creek.

Her memories of late last night had grown hazy.

She realized she was warm.

Her cheek rested against something soft.

What—?

She blinked and came fully awake.

She remembered lying down with her shoulder touching Collin's. For warmth.

Apparently, some time in the night, she'd turned toward him, curled into his side. Her head was firmly on his shoulder and—was that his arm around her?

She sat up, dislodging the saddle blanket from her midsection and his arm from around her. A hot blush blazed in her face. She drew her knees up to her chest as the chill of the morning seeped through her clothes, more noticeable now that she'd drawn away from Collin's warmth.

How humiliating.

He hummed as he came awake, probably because of her movement.

Maybe he didn't know that she'd been curled up against him like that. He'd been asleep, too, hadn't he?

He sat up, stretching his arms over his head. He was still much too close, and she couldn't help noticing how the material of his shirt stretched across his muscular chest.

She resolutely averted her face.

She'd told Lily that she wanted to marry someday.

But today was not that day.

And Collin was not that man.

Back in Dublin, she'd been invisible, always dressed in men's garb, one of the factory workers.

No one saw her.

On the steamer, dressed as herself again, she'd caught a single admiring look from a young man. She hadn't done anything about it, of course, but it had made her wonder.

Would God provide the right husband for her?

Someone to provide for her. To rub her shoulders after a long day of labor. Someone she could laugh with. Depend on.

She had a difficult time imagining it. Father hadn't been dependable. He'd relied on her to look after Maddie and Lily since they were small. He drank away his earnings, leaving her no choice but to put food on the table in other ways.

She didn't know whether she could do it. Really trust a

man to be her true partner. Not after being the one to take responsibility for so long.

Not even for someone like Collin.

The thought of him in that role—a romantic role— unnerved her. She must've made some noise because she sensed him look over at her.

"All right?" he asked. "Did you sleep at all?"

She nodded jerkily. "I—"

She stood up, startling him and breaking off her sentence. Her saddle blanket dropped to the ground unceremoniously, and she took several steps toward a sapling on the creek bank.

"What's that?" Collin asked from behind her. She heard the rustle of his clothing.

She bent over the young tree, touching its bark just below the small backward L that had been carved into it.

It was fresh.

"Lily left us a sign." She straightened, already glancing around to find the next one.

He brushed past her to squat in front of the sapling. "How do you know it's her?" he asked dubiously.

"When she was small and learning her letters, she would draw her L's backwards. It's hers."

He remained skeptical. "Or the storm knocked something into the tree and made that cut in the bark."

She caught sight of another backwards L and loped toward it, several yards down the creek bank. "Here's another."

He stared at her from where he stood, a dozen feet away.

Her heart pounded with joy and relief. She didn't even care that she probably looked a sight. Grubby and dirty from a night spent outdoors with no chance to wash up.

She reached up to gently touch the bandage they'd wrapped around her head to hide her hair. Had it come loose? Slipped? It seemed all right to her.

He glanced away, color rising into his face. "I'll start saddling up."

"Collin."

He hesitated.

"You were right. To make us take the time to rest last night. I was so sleepy I would've missed the sign completely."

His expression changed into an easy smile. He winked. "Could you say that to Leo when we get back to camp? *Collin was right.*"

Something passed over his expression. He didn't wait for her answer to his teasing statement. He strode back to where they'd passed a few hours in the night and gathered up his saddle and blanket.

Not for the first time, she realized he hadn't been able to check on his family yet. He'd been so busy helping her that he didn't know whether his siblings were all right.

It made an uncomfortable knot lodge in her belly. She owed him so much.

He helped her saddle up the stallion, who seemed unsettled this morning. Collin fed him peppermint candy from his saddlebag, but he remained restless. Maybe because they'd been separated from the camp all night?

Funny how she felt rested, unlike that first night alone with Collin where she'd been full of uncertainty. When had things changed between them?

She got into the saddle, hung on even as the stallion took a couple of steps to the right. He hadn't bucked her off. This morning, that would do.

They could make friends later.

She and Collin followed the signs carved into trees. Some were more difficult to find, hidden beneath a branch laden with leaves. Hidden at the base of the tree. Two were so far apart that Stella feared she'd lost the trail completely.

Only a half hour had passed before she caught sight of the hunter green of Maddie's dress, half-hidden behind a wide maple tree.

"It's me," she called out.

Lily peeped her head out from behind another tree. She had her pistol drawn. When she caught sight of Stella, she wilted in relief, leaning one shoulder against the tree.

———

COLLIN FELT an urgency to get back and check on his family. More so as Stella embraced her sisters, attempting to keep him from seeing the tears she blinked back.

Of course he saw.

"Are you hurt?" Maddie asked.

Stella felt the bandage around her head with a little laugh. "No. It's hiding my hair."

"You want my hat?" Lily asked.

Stella shook her head. "Then you'd have need of the bandage."

She was a different person around her sisters. More open.

But he couldn't forget Stella's stark terror last night when she'd seen the footprints near her family's abandoned wagon.

"I think it's time for that shooting lesson, don't you?" he asked.

"What, now?" Stella asked, clearly distracted as she checked over her sisters.

He had to pull his gaze away from her.

He was afraid he was turning into Leo. About to start mooning over Stella. Earlier he'd found himself staring at her when she stood on the bank of that creek, lit up like a firecracker he'd once seen tested at the mill. Her eyes were bright even with her clothes rumpled from where they'd slept on the ground. He'd still been buzzing with the realization that she'd been tucked close beside him as they'd slept.

There was something about her that drew him like a moth to a flame, and it wasn't simply her outward beauty. She was brave and independent and smart. He liked her.

And thinking about her was easier than wondering whether his family was still alive.

Stella and Lily took out their weapons, holding them gingerly. Maddie asked if she could be a part of the lesson, and he agreed. Meanwhile, Irene sat herself down with her back to a tree, looking off into the distance.

"We won't actually shoot," he said. "Don't want to waste your ammunition and the sound might draw attention from the wagon train." *Or anyone else who might be out here.* He caught Stella's knowing gaze.

Lily held the six-shooter up in front of her, aiming away from all of them, into the trees.

"Your stance is all wrong," he said. "You're leaning too far back. If you shoot the gun like that, the recoil is going to kick you back and you'll fall on your hindquarters."

Lily shifted into a more natural stance, and Maddie looked to him as he demonstrated, his hands empty.

Stella still wasn't getting it. He took a couple of steps over to her. He put his hands on her hips from behind and gently pushed her forward in her stance. There was a fine tension between them, but he tried to ignore it as he adjusted her grip on the gun and then moved his hands up her arms to adjust her shoulders.

He heard her soft intake of air.

Felt a little breathless himself at her nearness.

Forced himself to take a step back and look at her with a critical eye. "That's better."

"It feels unnatural."

"The more you practice it, the more you'll get used to it."

He glanced over and found Maddie with her nose wrinkled up and one eye closed as she tried to sight the gun. "You've got to keep both eyes open."

He moved two steps toward Lily, who seemed to have the knack of it. "She all right?" He nodded to Irene.

Lily shook her head. "She has been jumpy as a barn cat inside a house ever since..." She trailed off, glancing quickly at Stella.

Stella nodded. "I told him. I had no choice. Someone— a man—was nosing around our wagon after the rain came through."

Irene apparently didn't like hearing that at all. She stood, clutching her skirt nervously. One hand rested over her heart.

"We'll get back to the wagon train as quickly as we can," he said. "It'll be safer with more folks around."

But Irene didn't seem convinced.

He couldn't wait any longer. He needed to know if his family was all right.

He put Maddie and Irene on his horse and he walked. Stella and Lily rode the stallion. The animal sidestepped at the extra weight on its back. It was clear that whatever truce had been made between him and Stella, the stallion wasn't cooperating with her now.

"We'll find someone who can help us repair that wagon wheel of yours," he told Stella, because he knew she was still worrying about it.

"Do you think there even is a camp?" Maddie asked.

It was clear that the storm had shaken all of them.

"I'm sure they've started reorganizing," he said.

But his easy confidence might have been misplaced. When they arrived to a misshapen and miserable circle of wagons, things were in an uproar.

Raised voices sounded across the prairie, and while some folks were huddled near their wagons, a group of a few men stood in the center of the wagons with arms akimbo and high color in their faces. What was going on?

Collin was scanning the wagons. Alice happened to see him first. She said something to Leo, standing a few feet in front of her, clearly listening to the men who were arguing.

Leo caught Collin's eye and nodded, relief clear in his expression.

He stayed where he was while Alice rushed toward Collin.

He braced himself as she threw her whole body at him, wrapping her arms around his shoulders. "We were so worried about you!"

"I'm perfectly fine." She didn't seem to want to let him go, so he patted her back. He was aware of Stella and her family behind him, watching. "What about you? Any injuries? Where's Coop?"

"It missed us, but not by much."

Relief blitzed through him. It had missed them.

Alice was shaking, and now he realized she was crying.

"Hey. It's all right."

She shook her head, pushing back from his embrace. She pointed at a row of quilt-wrapped bundles, large ones, in the center of the circled wagons. "Coop and Leo spent all night out searching for you. Owen and August, too. Coop's still out there. August saw you race off just before the twister landed, and we thought—we thought—"

All of a sudden, he realized what the quilt-wrapped bundles were. Bodies. He counted six.

Alice watched the realization settle over him, her eyes wet and filled with pain.

He took her back in his arms. "I'm all right. I'm sorry I scared you."

He'd been worried about his family. He hadn't given enough consideration to the fact that they might be worrying about him. Frightened for his very life.

"Is Evangeline all right? Sara?"

Alice nodded, finally calming to the point where she pushed back from his hug and tried to mop up her face with her apron. "They're fine. The cattle are gone. Scattered to who knows where."

He felt a moment of regret that he hadn't been able to help in the moment the storm had come through.

Alice frowned at him. "Where were you?"

"Your brother saved my life." Stella had never spoken to Alice before as far as he knew. His sister looked surprised at the interruption. Stella took a tentative step closer. He caught her uncertain look as she glanced between him and Alice. "He helped me find my sisters and my aunt, and we're all grateful."

Alice was sharp. Her eyes flicked between him and the Fairfax family.

He didn't want her examining Stella too closely.

"Are there still folks missing?" he asked.

Alice nodded. "Owen's been organizing search parties. Some folks have started taking stock of what's left. Trying to find missing things that blew away. Make repairs to their wagons."

"Our wagon has a broken wheel," Stella said.

"They'll need help to repair it. It's a ways back," Collin said. "I can talk to Owen," he said to Stella.

Raised voices snagged Collin's attention. The men opposite Leo were arguing loudly and Leo had taken a couple steps closer. He wasn't captain any more, but Collin knew he'd keep the peace if possible.

"Owen's too busy to help you," Alice cautioned. "He's got August using all his tracking skills." She lowered her voice. "Hollis is missing."

TEN

Collin had spent most of the past twenty-four hours believing that all he had to do was get Stella and her sisters and Irene back to camp and they'd find safety there.

But this didn't feel safe.

The men in front of the Stewarts' wagon were getting louder.

After Alice had realized neither he nor the Fairfaxes had eaten all day, she'd promptly given them all cups of coffee and began finding them something to eat.

He sort of thought she wanted a moment to calm down after her teary outburst when he'd appeared.

Now Stella and Lily, dressed as men, sat near the campfire with steaming mugs of coffee in hand. Irene had shrank back into a shadow between the two wagons, maybe hoping to escape from notice there. Maddie had spotted someone with a gash in their forehead lying next to a fire across the ring of wagons and had rushed off, ignoring Stella's quiet order for her to stay nearby.

Maddie might not be formally trained, but she had a physician's heart. If someone was hurt or sick, she couldn't stand by and do nothing.

Neither could he. Stella was worried about a strange man in camp. He let his gaze scan everyone in the circle. Dozens of men, but he thought he recognized all of them.

It didn't stop Stella's gaze from flitting here, there, and everywhere, when he happened to glance in her direction. She still wore his makeshift bandage around her head, though it was hanging down over one ear. He needed to find her a hat.

He sidled up to Leo, not sure what he was going to say. How could he convince his brother to help protect Stella and her family without revealing her secret?

But Leo was intently focused on the man striding across camp.

Clarence Turnbull, one of the men who'd been elected a leader in their company.

Then Owen appeared in the gap between two wagons and hurried into camp. He looked both fierce and worn, but turned his steps toward them. Collin had never seen him anything other than put together, but today his trousers had a ragged rip in them and a bruise colored his jaw. Along with two days of stubble, he had tired lines around his eyes.

He met them just as Clarence reached Leo.

Leo stood with his hands loosely at his sides. Collin crossed his arms over his chest. And Owen put his hands on his hips. They were formidable, the three of them.

And Clarence suddenly looked reluctant. He glanced over his shoulder to the group of five men standing with their arms crossed, postures demanding.

"What d'you want, Clarence?"

Collin had never heard Leo speak in such a rude tone.

"There's a few of us that are ready to move on." The uncertainty in Clarence's voice made it unclear whether he was really one of them.

"We haven't located Hollis yet," Owen said steadily. "No use movin' until we've got our wagon master back."

"Some of 'em think Hollis abandoned us. And the fort's only a day's ride. Maybe a day and a half."

Leo shook his head. "Hollis wouldn't do that."

Collin agreed with his brother wholeheartedly. Back in Independence, Hollis had a reputation as the best wagon master there was. Hollis knew the land. And he knew men. He'd instituted safety measures—like the captain and his committee—meant to protect the travelers, even from themselves.

But apparently, since the storm had passed, folks had grown desperate. And fear wasn't a good companion to desperation.

"I know the fort is close, but we've got power in our numbers." Owen spoke in a reasonable tone. "The more men we've got looking for Hollis, the sooner we'll find him."

A couple of the men had edged closer and now a man Collin recognized as Elroy Jenkins called out to them. "He's dead!"

Collin was startled by his shout. The words more than the tone.

"If he's alive, why isn't he back?" Clarence rushed the words, his voice uneven.

Owen lowered his volume. "We don't know. He could be injured. Could need our help. We gotta find him."

Clarence looked as if he wanted to agree. Until another strident voice called out from behind him.

"We ain't stayin'. We got no food. Storm ruined it all."

Collin's compassion for the man and his family rose.

Leo jerked his chin. Collin followed the motion. Was that someone hiding behind a wagon? Halfway between the group of troublemakers and Leo and Evangeline's wagon, the shadow moved again.

"My family will happily share our food supply with you," Leo said. He'd gone tense, but his voice was calm and steady. "We've got plenty."

"That ain't all you got plenty of!" A voice rang out.

"Yeah!" Another voice joined the first.

Now Clarence looked regretful. What did they mean?

"Get back by Alice," Leo said to Collin in a low voice.

The last thing he wanted to do was leave his brother standing out in the open, in such a vulnerable place, by himself.

But Leo's flashing eyes meant this wasn't the time for questions. Collin faded back toward their campfire, keeping one eye on the shadow creeping nearer, just outside the ring of wagons.

"Everyone knows your pretty lil wife is flush with cash." Collin couldn't see which man said it, as Leo and Owen, standing side-by-side, blocked his view. "It ain't fair that some of us lost everything and you got so much."

"If anyone in this company is thinking of taking what doesn't belong to them, I'll remind you of Hollis's rules. No thieving," Owen said.

"Hollis ain't here!" A voice shouted.

"We need to get to the fort and resupply!" The next one came right on the heels of the first.

And a shot rang out, echoing in the sudden stillness.

Collin strode the last two yards to put himself in front

of Alice and Evangeline, who were huddled together, Sara in Evangeline's arms. The little girl had put her hands over her ears. Her bottom lip trembled. Evangeline put her hand over Sara's head, holding her against her shoulder as if to shield her.

Stella stood, one hand at the revolver at her waist. Lily remained sitting by the fire but alert and watching everything. Her coffee cup had spilled on the ground, liquid seeping into the dirt.

Coop revealed himself, rifle in hand. He swept the weapon in a sideways motion. A short man with a barrel chest and a scraggly beard stepped out of the shadows. He had a gun in the belt at his waist but his arms were up in the air and his face was white.

"That was a warning shot," Coop said, voice clear in the silent camp. "But you only get one warning."

"My wife and I will share a meal with anyone who's hungry," Leo said. His voice was hard now. "We'll help you however we can. But no one is stealing from us."

"Or anyone else," Owen added.

Clarence said something to the two men that Collin couldn't hear. He hoped it was an apology.

Coop waved off the man who'd been sneaking around and trudged across the camp in full view of everyone. What had been the man's intentions? Even Collin didn't know where Evangeline and Leo had hidden her money. From what he knew about her, he doubted the wagon was loaded down with gold coins. She probably had bank notes somewhere, and what were any of them going to do with those out here in the wilderness?

He hoped someone could talk some sense into these desperate men.

He glanced over and found Stella's gaze on him. He'd promised her his help, but he hadn't counted on his family needing him too.

———

STELLA WATCHED realization come over Collin. He was so open. He didn't hide anything that he felt.

What must it be like to live that free? To not have to hide all the time?

She'd forgotten.

Or maybe she'd never known.

Collin wasn't going to be able to help repair her wagon wheel. Not with his family being threatened. She'd realized it before he had.

She was disappointed, but quickly pushed it away. She shouldn't have leaned on him. Shouldn't have expected anything. Had she learned nothing from her father and every other man who had let her down?

If she wanted her wagon repaired, she was going to have to find a way to do that herself.

It was a good thing God had given her smarts.

"Where's Maddie?" Lily whispered.

Stella's gaze darted to the last place she'd seen her sister. Gone.

Her heart in her throat, she spun on her heel. Her stomach twisted in an anxious knot. She should've marched over and physically grabbed her sister, made her stay close—

There she was, on the heels of August Mason, who was striding into camp from the north. He was carrying an unconscious young woman in his arms while another woman, looking rumpled and tired, trailed behind him. Stella had seen the pair of them before. They took turns driving. The one with dark hair in braids and medium brown skin always cooked. And the one with pale skin and brown hair was often seen at the water, washing their clothes or dishes.

She'd seen Hollis take a special interest in their wagon but hadn't known why.

When it was apparent August was heading in their direction, she motioned to Lily to vacate the fire.

Alice had seen them coming and rushed to the cookpot on the ground near their wagon.

"She's bad hurt," August called out as he got close. "Wagon collapsed on top of her. She's got a bad cut at her throat."

"Put her in my tent," Evangeline called out.

August changed course slightly to head for the white tent erected next to their wagon.

Stella's gaze met Maddie's worried one. "How can I help?" she asked.

"I don't know," Maddie said. "We'll need a lot of hot water."

August couldn't fit inside the tent while he was standing, so he knelt awkwardly in the entrance. His back was to Stella and she couldn't see much, but she saw him gently lay the injured woman inside.

Alice appeared at his side. She glanced at the woman who'd been following him.

"I'm Abigail Barton," the woman said.

"Alice Spencer."

"You a praying sort, Miss Alice?"

As Alice nodded, Stella found she had to look away

from the instant camaraderie between the two women, their similar determination.

Water. They needed water for the pot Alice had moved over the fire.

August had straightened, and apparently Leo had felt it safe to come away from his position guarding the wagon from the center of the circle.

Stella quickly moved to intercept him. August did the same.

The two men towered over her and she did her best to rise on her toes in her boots without making it obvious.

But then she stepped back as the two brothers, now standing a few feet away, obviously wanted to converse.

COLLIN STANDING NEXT to his brother Coop, noticed her from yards away. His eyes glittered, though his face betrayed no hint of a smile.

"What was that shot?" August asked.

Leo filled him in quickly. He glanced around their camp, his eyes skipping over Stella as if she wasn't there. He was checking on each member of his family, she realized.

She found herself watching Collin and Coop as they spoke in low tones. The two men had similar stances, identical jawlines, the same brown eyes. Coop wore a hat, and the men's shirts were different colors of blue. Other than that, they were identical.

But in a strange way, she thought she would know Collin even if they were dressed the same.

The difference was in the slight hardness to the set of Coop's eyes. Collin seemed more... decent, somehow.

He motioned to Coop with a whirl of his finger. Coop's brow wrinkled. What were they talking about?

"Can't believe I missed all the fun," August said, interrupting her thoughts.

She needed to stay focused. Allowing herself to be distracted by Collin was foolish.

Leo just looked grim. "We're going to have to set a watch." He shot a glance at Clarence and the men who'd dispersed. "I'm not so naive to think they've given up so easily. Desperate men make bad decisions."

The bitterness in his voice spoke of some experience he'd lived through.

This was her chance. She couldn't have asked for a better opening.

She cleared her throat. Pitched her voice low. "I'd like to help. For a trade."

Both Leo and August's stares landed on her. She almost quailed beneath them. Instead, she gritted her teeth and went on.

"Our wagon needs repairs. You need a coupla extra pairs of eyes to keep watch." She nodded to Lily then indicated herself with a wave of her gloved hand. "And I overheard Alice telling Collin that your cattle need rounding up. It'll be difficult to spare men for that if you need to keep your womenfolk safe. I can help."

Leo considered her while August looked a bit skeptical. Had he noticed how much difficulty she'd had handling the stallion?

She couldn't let August discount her riding skills. And the longer Leo thought about her offer, the more likely he was to say no, at least to her thinking.

She nodded to where the group of men had dispersed. "There were at least four men listening to the louder ones, who haven't decided a course of action yet. If they decide to add their guns to the others..."

Leo and his family would be vastly outnumbered.

His lips thinned. "We need to find Hollis," he said to August. Then he swung his gaze back to her. "It's a deal. We'll help you with the repair if you'll help us round up the missing cattle."

He didn't mention standing watch, but she'd insist on that, too. She wasn't going to take charity.

She nodded and moved off to tell Lily. Irene had been commandeered to heat the hot water at the stove, though she kept sending furtive glances around the camp.

Collin met Stella at the edge of the wagon.

"This is for you." He held out a brown felt hat.

She looked across the campsite and realized where he'd gotten it from. "That's your brother's hat."

"So it is. You can't wear that bandage forever. It's gonna slip, and then your hair will be loose."

She frowned. He was right, of course.

"I should've cut if off before," she murmured.

"No, you shouldn't have. It's too pretty to cut."

A moment passed between them, one where she couldn't seem to drag her gaze away from his. Her cheeks felt hot.

"You spend a lot of time taking care of your sisters," he said. "Who takes care of you?"

She didn't know how to answer him so she glanced away.

Coop, standing near the fire, talking with Leo, was staring right at her.

There was nothing untoward in Collin's stature, with that hat outstretched toward her. He was only as close as an acquaintance would stand.

But she didn't like the way Coop was watching. It made her nervous to have so many eyes on her.

She snatched the hat from Collin. "Thanks."

"You sure you want to ride out to find those cows?" he asked. "The stallion—"

"I'll take care of my own business," she said with a snap and walked off toward the stallion.

She shouldn't have spoken to him like that, not after he'd helped her so much.

But her heart was beating so hard she could feel it pounding in her temples. It was a risk, this burgeoning friendship with Collin. He had a family who cared about him, watched out for him.

How long before someone else figured out her ruse?

And maybe that person wouldn't be as understanding as Collin.

She'd seen the terror on her sisters' faces when she and Collin had finally found them in the woods. She was the responsible one. The one who'd risked all of their lives to come to America, who'd chosen this avenue of escape.

If she wasn't taking care of her sisters, who would? They had no one else.

She thought about it for a long time in the dark.

Father had never asked her to help watch over her sisters. He hadn't had to.

She could still remember being ten, him passed out in his bed in their small apartment. There'd been no food.

Lily had been tiny and crying because she was so hungry.

Stella had gone out into the street. Maybe she'd beg. Surely someone would help them.

No one had.

She'd stolen two apples from a grocer. And never been

caught. Never punished like Collin had been in the story he'd told about his brother.

At the time, she'd made the only choice she could.

And she'd do it all over again. For Lily and for Maddie.

But his words wouldn't leave her.

Who takes care of you?

ELEVEN

"Giddap, now."

Stella could hear Collin's order from where she sat atop the stallion as they walked their horses through the woods about a half mile from camp.

He must've found another cow. He seemed to have an uncanny knack for sniffing them out when they tried to hide in bramble patches and little gullies.

She could hear him, but she couldn't see him. They'd woken to a foggy mist in the air, the like of which she'd never seen before.

In camp, she had only been able to see the nearest two wagons. Everything across the circle had been blocked from view by the fog. Coop and August had been out most of the night, along with other search parties. Two more bodies had been recovered. Everyone was accounted for—except for Hollis. The company planned to have a joint funeral in the morning. She didn't know whether Owen would decide to move on or not after that. Surely they couldn't continue to stay out here indefinitely...

The fog dampened every sound and made her feel as if she was alone, though she knew Collin rode not far away.

Late yesterday afternoon, Collin and another man from camp, a carpenter by trade, had ridden out to repair and fetch her wagon. They'd rolled in well after dark, but it hadn't mattered.

Irene had been so emotional about having the wagon back that she'd been in tears as she thanked the two men. Maddie had come to fetch some of her herbs from inside and disappeared again, helping someone else who'd been injured. Lily had been on first watch, but when she'd returned, jaw cracking in a yawn, she'd nodded her approval.

And this morning, Stella was making good on her promise to help Collin and his brothers round up their cattle.

She wished she knew what she was doing.

The animals should be easy to spot. They were big, almost as big as her horse. Some black, some brown, they didn't exactly blend into the landscape. But with the fog hanging low over the ground, it was hard to see anything at all.

And the stallion seemed skittish. He'd been acting so all morning.

Even now, at a walk, he neighed and bobbed his head. She'd checked the bit and his mouth. His mouth had healed over the past days, and there were no signs of irritation in his teeth or gums or cheek. Why was he fighting her so much?

Be calm. She tried to remember Collin's admonishment from that first night.

But it was hard not to jump when the shifting fog revealed a dark tree stump that for one terrifying moment was the shape of a tall man.

She attempted to shake off the feeling that there were eyes watching her. Irene's fears were rubbing off on her. She'd watched every face in camp last night. There was no stranger among the company now, if there had ever been one.

The fog shifted again.

There.

A pair of reddish brown steers were grazing in a hollow near a wide sycamore tree.

Using her legs, she urged the stallion to approach them. She was supposed to push any cattle she ran across out into the open field, where Coop was holding them in a loose herd before they rode back to the wagon train. Collin was somewhere out to her left among the misty fog.

"Giddyap," she ordered the beasts.

One of them mooed at her.

The stallion side-stepped. She held her seat—barely—using the reins to try and control him as he spun halfway around.

One of the cows moved the direction she wanted him to go.

The other headed in the opposite direction at a trot.

No!

She tried to speed up the stallion to catch the ornery cow, but he shied again as the fog shifted.

She tried clucking at him, imitating the sound she'd heard one of the other travelers make at some point.

The stallion fought her, tossing its head. What was wrong with him, today? He was as nervous as Irene.

The stallion jumped ahead a long stride. She cried out, the sudden movement almost unseating her.

And then the stallion twisted. She didn't see the low-hanging tree branch until it was too late. The branch hit her midsection hard enough that a loud smack reverberated through the quiet morning.

Unceremoniously, she fell from the saddle and hit the ground hard, landing on her side.

She gasped for air, the wind knocked out of her by the branch. She gasped each little inhale but couldn't seem to take in any air. What was wrong with her?

Panic clawed at her throat as black spots danced at the edges of her vision. She tried to push up off the ground where she lay, but the lack of air had somehow sapped her strength and she couldn't.

And then sudden hoofbeats sounded. Close.

Fog swirled before a horse and rider appeared. Collin.

He was off the horse and kneeling at her side in an instant.

"What's the matter?" he demanded.

She couldn't catch her breath to tell him.

He gripped her upper arm, his eyes a little wild as he scanned her face. His lips firmed, and he gave her a quick thump on the center of her back.

Something loosened in her chest and breath exhaled noisily.

She drew the first sweet gulp of air and her muscles that had locked up went loose. She would've slumped to the ground, but he braced her with an arm behind her back.

Another breath. He was close enough that she could smell the soap he'd used to wash up with last night, and a whiff of his horse. His own scent, one she'd dreamed about last night after falling asleep with her head against his shoulder...

"What happened?" he asked.

She caught sight of the stallion standing with reins dragging the ground only a few yards away.

Her voice was rough when she tried to speak. She had to clear her throat. "Something spooked him. He whirled around and the branch caught me."

He flicked a glance overhead and when he looked back to her, concern etched his expression. "Did you crack a rib? How hard did you hit? Your face was so pale—"

She cut him off with a gentle hand against his chest. His eyelashes had matted together in the wet air. His hair curled at his forehead and neck.

He'd gone still. Now he looked down at her gloved hand. Back up into her face. Some indecision flickered across his expression, then resolved itself into a look of determination.

She only got to admire the expression for a moment before he leaned in and kissed her.

His lips were cool and firm. Maybe she'd knocked her hat loose in that fall or maybe he did when his hand slid into her hair, his fingers scraping against her scalp in the most pleasurable way.

She'd never kissed anyone before—never had the chance. But he seemed pleased as she gently pressed herself into the kiss, as she returned his tender touch by curling her hand around the nape of his neck.

He drew away, but not by much. His nose was still pressed against her cheek and his warm breaths puffed against her cheek.

"You scared me," he whispered, and she felt the words against her skin.

"Didn't mean to."

His head tipped toward her and she knew he was going to kiss her again. Her heart was pounding. It almost drowned out the sound of distant hoofbeats.

"Collin?" Coop's voice carried through the mist. Not close enough to see them yet.

But she scrambled away, her side aching when she got to her feet. She quickly reached for the hat as her hair tumbled around her shoulders.

Collin must've loosened her pins with his touch.

He stared at her even as he answered his brother. "Just a minute."

COLLIN COULDN'T STOP STARING at Stella.

She'd shied away like an unbroken filly when Coop had called out. Collin wasn't as worried. Coop was still a ways off.

Good thing, too.

With the color high in her cheeks and her lips pink and beestung like they were... Coop would take one look and realize that Stella wasn't Stephen after all.

How had Collin ever been stupid enough to look at her and see a man?

Her arms were raised as she tucked her hair under that hat, and he couldn't stop the raucous pounding of his heart, couldn't stop thinking about how she'd felt in his arms.

He wanted to kiss her again.

But now wasn't the time. Would there be a time for them?

"Are you sure you're all right?" he asked. "Want me to—"

"No," she said quickly.

She didn't even know what he was going to say.

She turned away and slipped off through the swirling mist. He saw the outline of her stallion as Coop's hoofbeats drew closer.

Stella stepped up into the saddle and moved off as Coop appeared through the fog, tall in the saddle.

He didn't look surprised to see Collin standing on the ground instead of on his horse.

"What're you doing?" Coop asked. He glanced in the direction Collin had last seen Stella, but she was already gone. "Stretching your legs?"

Collin was grateful for the suggestion, because his mind had slipped back to the press of Stella's lips against his. It wasn't an outright lie. Being out of the saddle was stretching his legs. "Uh, yeah."

"By yourself?" Coop prodded. "I thought I heard voices from this direction."

Collin spread his hands. "You see anyone else?" Now he was grateful for the chance to turn his back for a moment to walk the few steps to his horse. He felt his face flame at the subterfuge. He didn't like it.

How did Stella live like this? Constantly choosing one's words carefully. White lies.

It's why she and the other Fairfaxes kept their distance from everyone, he realized. Collin had thought them stand-offish. Unfriendly. But Stella had just been trying to stay out of people's notice.

It'd been a risk for her to strike that deal with Leo. Exchange help. Bring her family close enough so they were under his family's protection—sort of.

His saddle creaked as he threw his leg over and settled into the leather.

Coop was still watching his every move with hooded eyes. "You sure you didn't get hit on the head when that storm came through? You been actin' strange. Distracted."

His horse must've sensed the rising tension inside him because its ears flicked.

"I didn't get hit in the head," he confirmed.

"Something going on between you and Stephen Fairfax? That greenhorn making trouble for you?"

He didn't know why his brother was so concerned right now. They had a job to do. Leo and Alice were counting on them.

There was a part of him that wanted to tell Coop everything. He *liked* Stella. Prickles and independent spirit and all.

But the thought of what Coop had put the family through in recent weeks sobered him right up and kicked that idea out of his brain.

Stella wanted to keep her true identity, and Lily's, hidden. Right or wrong, she'd chosen her path.

If Coop let the truth slip... Collin couldn't bear it if his brother was the reason she was found out.

Coop hadn't had a drop to drink since James Murphy had died—that anyone knew about. But Collin didn't trust his white-knuckled hold on his sobriety. He'd gone dry for periods before.

Didn't mean it was going to stick.

And as much as he hated to think it, he wasn't sure he could trust his brother.

He'd been cleaning up after him for too long. This thing with Stella had shown him that much.

"Nothing's going on," he lied.

He didn't like it, but it was better to keep his brother in the dark. For now.

Judging by Coop's skeptical expression, he was going to have to keep a distance from Stella in camp. He didn't think he was a skilled enough liar to keep his twin from seeing his feelings for her written across his face.

"Better get back to the herd," he murmured.

Coop stared at him for a long moment, then slowly wheeled his horse, sending one glance back. His expression had closed off. For once, Collin couldn't tell what Coop was thinking.

"Twelve more steers missing," he said.

"Hopefully the fog will burn off and we'll find them in one big bunch," Collin responded.

Coop shook his head and rode off.

Collin had said the words to get rid of his brother. He didn't feel particularly positive toward Coop right now.

He wanted things to be different. Wanted to be able to trust Coop.

But he couldn't.

Before Stella, before he'd known how deeply he could care about her—deeper than friendship, that was sure—he would've said he was holding out hope that things between him and Coop could still be repaired.

Leo had given up on Coop. And Coop appeared to be working hard to get back in his good graces.

But Collin couldn't help wondering if it would last.

That meant you got whipped on your birthday. Stella's words from days ago crept into his mind.

He hadn't thought about it the way she had, not until she'd said the words. *You took his punishment.*

He'd been trying to protect his brother.

Something that Coop didn't seem to appreciate. Had he ever said thank you after any of the numerous times

Collin had gotten him out of this scrape or that? Collin couldn't remember a time.

He did remember those lashes he'd taken. And the guilt he'd taken on after New Jersey.

He still felt it, pulsing beneath his skin.

Did Coop care about the things Collin had done for him?

Collin didn't think he could keep on going the way they had been.

TWELVE

You're lucky to be alive.

Felicity didn't remember who had said the words. After August and Abigail had found her, things had been a blur of pain. She'd slipped out of consciousness as August carried her back to camp.

She didn't feel lucky.

She was covered in bruises, but it was the invisible damage to her midsection that was most worrisome. When she used the necessary—with copious help from Abigail— there was blood in her urine.

She'd broken two ribs on the left side of her body and had ugly yellow and purple bruises all up and down that side of her body. Her arm was splinted.

And she still couldn't speak.

She had been the quiet one in a noisy family her entire life. She'd—mostly—happily faded into the background. She'd *never* been chatty.

But now that she was physically unable to speak, she found she had never wanted something so badly.

Felicity was lying on a pallet inside Alice Spencer's tent. She'd been in here all day, with the tent flaps open, watching what she could see of the comings and goings in camp.

The search for Hollis continued and now the sun was going down again. Men on horseback kept reporting back to camp in pairs or trios. No one had found any sign of him.

What would they do without a wagon master?

There was movement near the Spencers' wagon. It was Alice, who'd been in and out of the temporary campsite all day. Abigail, too. They'd cooked food for some of the families who had suffered damage to their wagons and supplies. Helped repair the canvas cover for another wagon. Watched little ones as mothers and fathers sought to set things to rights.

Felicity wanted nothing more than to help them. Work would quiet the swirling thoughts she was stuck with hour after hour. And helping with repairs was the least she could do after the Spencers and the Mason brothers had taken in her and Abigail, their wagon decimated by the twister. But her injuries prevented her from being any real help.

It seemed Alice was back now. Maybe to cook supper for her own family? Abigail was nowhere in sight.

But then another person joined Alice near the fire she was stoking.

August.

Before the terrible storm, Felicity had fancied him in the same way she'd fancied other men—from a distance and in a silent way that they'd never guess. She hadn't even known his name.

And now her injuries trapped her in his campsite.

He smiled at Alice. She made a gesture toward the wagon, and he moved to the rear of it. Pointed to something inside the wagon bed that Felicity couldn't see. Alice called out an affirmative.

Something inside Felicity twisted at the sight of them together.

Were they...? Was August her beau?

Felicity was so timid that she'd only really made friends with Abigail. And that had been hard enough. She'd watched the other travelers from the seat of the wagon. Or in camp, by casting, furtive glances as she toted wood for the fire as Abigail cooked.

She'd gathered there was some connection between the Masons and Spencers. They often parked their wagons side-by-side in the big circle. She'd caught some tension between the menfolk. Was this why? Because August was sweet on Alice?

Alice said something to him. Felicity couldn't quite hear. His head turned and he caught sight of her inside the tent.

Her face flamed to be the recipient of his notice.

She'd been invisible until Alice had pointed out her presence.

She averted her eyes from him but it didn't seem to matter, because he approached. She could hear each of his footsteps hit the ground. And then he was leaning over the tent entrance to see inside, his body casting a long shadow inside.

"Howdy, Miss Felicity. How are you?"

She nodded in answer and saw his brows shift in concern.

"Your throat still paining you?"

She nodded again. Even if she'd had words, she wasn't sure she'd be able to explain it. Every time she swallowed, her throat felt swollen, just on the edge of pain. But when she tried to speak—even a whisper—pain sliced through her throat like a knife.

His gaze took her in. She was aware of the borrowed dress, the bruising on her bare arms, and the splint. She hadn't seen a looking glass to know if her face was as battered as the rest of her.

"You been in here all day?" he asked gently. "Want to get out for a bit? I'll help ya."

When she nodded again, he bent to slide one arm around her back. She could feel the muscles of his arm flex. She tried to focus on that instead of the searing pain in her side and ribs.

She mustn't have masked it well, because he stopped when she was upright, just went completely still with his arm now around her waist and most of her weight leaning on him.

"Hurts that bad?" He looked down into her face, his blue eyes shadowed with concern.

My, he was close. Here in the curve of his arm, she felt protected by the width of his shoulders. And a little unsettled. She'd never been this close to a man who wasn't her father.

I'm fine. She mouthed the words, not knowing whether or not he would understand.

"No, you ain't."

She didn't want his pity.

She pulled away from the comfort of his arm around her. Each step shot arrows of pain through her, but she was determined to prove she wasn't weak.

"All right." There was a tone of exasperation in his voice. It only took him a step to catch up to her. He took her elbow in his big hand, and she was grateful for his support because the pain in her side was almost unbearable.

He helped her sit on a barrel near the fire. Alice was chopping what looked like a potato on the wagon bed.

Can I help? The words weren't audible, and what could she have done anyway, in her condition?

Having something to do with her hands would not only make her feel useful, it would provide a kind of comfort. A familiar one.

As the oldest in a household of eight children, she'd borne the most responsibility. At times, she'd rebelled against it. She'd wanted the freedom to read a book or lie on her bed and daydream. Not constant chores.

And now she'd been lying in bed all day and dreaming of doing chores.

August stood nearby, looking as if he wasn't quite sure what he was supposed to be doing. "That's a pretty dress," he said.

It's not mine. She mouthed the words again, but he shook his head. He didn't understand.

Alice glanced over from where she was working. "It's a borrowed dress, Auggie."

Auggie. If she'd asked for a sign that the two were close, there it was. Her heart sank inside her.

"How come?"

This time it was Alice's voice tinged with exasperation. "Everyone's been busy searching for Hollis and any other survivors. No one's been out to retrieve her things from the wagon."

August's expression turned thoughtful. Felicity had to look away. She stared at the crackling fire.

She had been in terrible pain when August and Abigail had rescued her. She remembered snatches. The wagon had been destroyed. Was there anything *to* salvage?

She and Abigail had made the wagon their home. It

wasn't ideal, but it was something. Abigail had kept a tiny posy of wildflowers tied with a ribbon to a nail inside the wagon. Felicity had organized all their supplies and kept everything tidy.

It hadn't been much. But it'd been theirs.

She'd saved for three years to take this journey.

And now all of her supplies and the wagon she'd depended on were gone.

The smoke from the fire suddenly made her throat burn. That's all it was, not tears.

Or maybe tears.

August shifted from foot to foot, looking uncomfortable now.

"When there's time, I'll go out and see what can be saved," he said.

That was kind of him, but she was afraid it was a lost cause.

THIRTEEN

It took all day, but they found all but two of the Spencers' cows. It was a hard loss, a monetary one that Stella was sorry for. The storm hadn't left the Spencer family unscathed after all.

The sun was setting as they pushed the herd back to where the company had made camp, Stella kept as much distance between herself and Collin as possible. For the most part, she kept the entire herd between them.

She kept replaying their kiss in her mind.

And she'd come to the only possible conclusion.

It couldn't happen again. She had to stay away from him.

His kiss was... dangerous. She'd liked it far too much.

She'd lost herself in his touch. Lost any sense of propriety, of where she was. Coop could've ridden right up on them and she'd been so lost to passion that she wouldn't have known.

Collin had helped her immensely.

She liked *him*.

But her sisters' survival depended on her. Her own happiness, her own desires would have to wait.

And it wasn't fair to him to pretend something could grow between them when it was impossible.

Back at camp, Collin stayed with the herd while Coop rode in to camp to talk to Leo.

They didn't need Stella any more. She'd only just dismounted her horse when she felt all of it catch up to her. The long nights and the terror of the storm and the uncertainty of not knowing whether her sisters were all right...

All of it hit her at once, and she was grateful for the stallion's height. She hid behind him, the wagon at her back, as she moved to unsaddle him, allowing herself one moment to duck her head, one moment to try and stem the exhausted tears gathering in her eyes.

She was so tired. Tired of running, of constantly looking over her shoulder, of searching for home.

"You look plumb worn out." The female voice came from too close. Stella quickly worked to blink away her tears, still hidden by the brim of her hat shading her face.

She straightened her shoulders and hefted the saddle off the horse. Looking up, she saw Alice Spencer standing by the nearest tent, an empty plate in her hand. Stella knew there'd been a young woman grievously injured, and Alice and Maddie and the Spencers were taking care of her.

Alice looked at Stella with concern.

This was the uncomfortable thing about parking their wagon so close to the Spencers and Masons. No privacy. She hadn't erected her wall of crates the way she'd done before. Too tired.

"Food's still warm. I can make you a plate. You've got first watch, right?"

She knew Alice was just trying to be neighborly, but

the words made Stella want to cry all over again. She'd forgotten about going on watch. She wanted to curl up in her bedroll beneath the wagon and fall into a dreamless sleep.

But she'd made a deal with Leo, brought Maddie and Irene and even Lily under his protection. There was safety in numbers, and the unrest in camp had made it necessary. She wasn't going to go back on her word. No matter how much she wanted to sleep.

She lifted the saddle back onto the stallion. "I'll eat later. I'd better check on my—on my siblings." She almost forgot to deepen her voice.

She'd almost slipped and said *sisters*. That itself was a sign of how exhausted she was. She needed to be careful.

Alice seemed content with her answer. Since Stella was going to have to ride again shortly, she patted the stallion's shoulder. "Sorry, fella. We've still got work to do."

He ignored her, lipping some of the grasses within his reach.

She didn't know what had been wrong with him earlier. He seemed fine, not jumpy at all, during the afternoon.

Maddie appeared from around the side of the wagon. When she glimpsed Stella, relief crossed her expression. She beckoned her closer.

"Irene's sick," she murmured.

Stella rolled her eyes. Irene was using that ruse again? "Where's Louis?"

"Went to the creek."

Probably washing up. Stella hoped Lily was careful.

"Irene's not faking this time," Maddie said, and Stella registered the urgency in her voice.

Maddie seemed to want her to follow, so Stella trailed

her to the wagon and climbed up into the wagon box behind her.

Maddie loosened the canvas and then moved out of the way so Stella could lean inside.

Irene was lying on the pallet she'd made inside the wagon weeks ago, when she'd only been pretending to be sick. Her face was flushed and lines of pain fanned around her mouth, though she seemed to be sleeping. One arm was crossed over her midsection.

Stella turned her head to whisper to Maddie, "What's wrong with her?"

"Fever, some vomiting. She can't keep any water down. It might be... someone from one of the other wagons said it could be cholera." Maddie barely breathed the word, as if she was afraid just saying it might make it true.

Irene moaned and tossed her head but didn't rouse.

"You aren't sick, are you?" Stella demanded in a low voice. She popped her head out of the wagon and scanned the nearby landscape. Where was Lily? Was she feeling sick?

Cholera was dangerous. Everyone on the wagon train knew how it could spread. It could be deadly.

Stella's stomach pinched and she knew a moment of unease—but it was only the worry for her sisters making her hurt.

"Stella..." Maddie's urgent whisper brought her head whipping back.

Maddie hadn't called her by her real name in weeks.

She followed Maddie's gaze back into the wagon. Sometime before now, Irene had loosened the neck of her dress. Probably the fever had made her want to get cool air on her skin.

Now, something glittered against her skin, barely visible above the neckline of her dress.

"What is that?" Maddie breathed.

It was big. Stella could tell from the outline of it.

She leaned farther into the wagon and reached out, using just her fingertips to nudge the... *necklace* into plain view.

It was more than a necklace, that much was obvious when it slipped out to lay on the rumpled blanket beneath Irene.

It was the biggest stone Stella had ever laid eyes on. A sparkling deep red that she couldn't seem to look away from. It must be a ruby. It was shaped like a heart, and she was pretty sure those were diamonds encrusted around the exterior of it. It was on a gold chain, attached to Irene.

Stella felt Maddie pressing in against her side, probably trying to get a glimpse—

Maddie gasped softly, and it was at that sound that Irene's eyes flew open. Her eyes were hazy with fever, but she gripped Stella's wrist with surprising force.

"It's mine," Irene growled fiercely.

It had to be worth a bucketload of money.

Stella couldn't imagine a woman living in the awful tenement apartments owning a piece of jewelry like this. It didn't make sense.

And then she remembered the leather pocketbook that had been inside the safe that Irene had cracked. Stella had been keeping lookout, her back turned to the safe as she'd stared out into the hallway. She had glanced over her shoulder once Irene got the safe open. There'd been piles of cash... and that leather folder tied with a strap.

"Did you steal it?" she demanded in a whisper.

"They *owed* me," Irene spat, her eyes wild. "They took the best years of my life, used me up—"

She moaned, pressing one hand against her stomach. Then she curled into a ball, giving Stella her shoulder.

It wasn't a straight answer, but Stella knew the truth with a dreadful certainty.

Irene had stolen that priceless jewel from the Byrne brothers.

COLLIN WAS in the saddle near the herd, talking to Leo who'd walked out from camp.

The sun was setting, casting a golden glow over everything, and all he could think about was having Stella tucked close to his side on a beautiful night like this.

He saw a slim, solitary figure walking back to camp from a wooded place a quarter mile off. For a moment, his mind played a trick on him, told him it was Stella, even though he'd seen her ride her stallion toward camp.

It must be Lily, in trousers and with that hat clapped low over her brow.

From his saddle, he watched the group of three men slink out of the shadows of the circle of wagons and approach her.

"Leo," he warned.

His brother followed his nod, though he couldn't have as good a view over the backs of the milling steers as Collin did.

Lily's easy gait had gone stiff when the men approached.

Collin couldn't hear what they said to her, they were too far away, but her shoulders went tense.

The three men surrounded her, though they hadn't moved closer than a few feet.

"I'm going—" Collin started, but Leo was already running around the mob of steers toward the four people.

Collin urged his horse into a gallop and quickly outpaced his brother.

Coop and Owen must've heard something from inside the circle of wagons, because here they came too.

Unfortunately, so did Clarence Turnbull and three other men with malice in their expressions.

Collin slid off his horse, sending dust flying.

"You threw in your lot with the Spencers—" One of the men was spitting mad, his fury directed at Lily, who was pale beneath her hat.

From the corner of his eye, he caught sight of Stella in camp. She was in the wagon bed but jumped off. Ran toward the gathering of men that was quickly becoming dangerous.

No. He didn't want her mixed up in this.

Collin stepped in front of Lily. "What seems to be the problem?"

He must not have gotten the peacemaker tone quite right, because the man stepped closer, now in Collin's face. "We wasn't speakin' to you."

Some spittle flew out of the man's mouth and landed on Collin's cheek. His temper rumbled, demanding payback for the disgusting slight.

"Hey!" Leo shouted, but he was still several yards away. Owen and Coop, too.

Stella's wagon had been parked the closest—Lily was heading for it when she'd been coming back. Which meant she was closer than the others when she'd hopped down. He stared at the man in front of him, two inches taller than Collin, face flushed with temper, and maybe drink.

Collin willed Stella away.

But she didn't stop her approach.

"Stay away from the Fairfax family," Collin said.

"Or else what?" the man standing behind Lily asked, laughter in his voice. "They got a wagon full of supplies and two puny menfolk. We all know they ain't got the gumption to protect themselves—"

"That's enough." Owen's voice rang out from outside the group of men, but Clarence stopped him before he got close to Collin.

"We need to work together, not be at each others' throats," Owen said.

The man in front of Collin spat in the dirt at his feet. "You thinkin' you're gonna be wagon master? Cuz I ain't followin' you nowhere."

Clarence had put his hand on Owen's arm. Maybe to stop him from walking forward.

Owen shrugged off his touch.

And Clarence gave him a shove.

Stella pushed past the man nearest her. Collin realized she was angling to push next to Lily, who still hovered uncertainly behind him.

But the man must've thought Stella wanted a fight, because he grabbed her arm and whirled her around.

Collin shouted, saw the fist coming toward her even as the man in front of him pulled his arm back.

Stella ducked and sort of backed into her assailant at the last second, and the punch bounced off her shoulder.

Collin wasn't as lucky. He'd been so distracted by her that he got clocked in the jaw, hard enough to ring his bell and make him see stars.

Then a sudden surprised shout.

"She's a woman!"

The man who'd been scuffling with him pulled away. When he moved, Collin had a clear view of Stella's hat, knocked to the ground.

She'd been knocked down too. She sat bracing her hands behind her, blonde hair cascaded down her shoulders.

The men had stopped fighting as shock and confusion broke the tensions of the moment.

Behind Collin, a man stepped forward. Collin didn't have time to intercept him as he whipped Lily's hat off her head.

"This one's a girl too."

Lily's hair stayed pinned up, but without her hat on, her fine cheekbones and those doe eyes made it pretty clear that she wasn't a teenaged boy.

Stella's cheek was scraped. Had Stewart gotten a punch in after all?

Collin wanted to kill him. As he took a step that direction, Stella glanced at him.

There was naked fear in her eyes, and he had a visceral reaction to it.

"Leave them alone," he demanded as she scrambled to her feet and toward him.

He gripped her upper arm and could feel her shaking. She snaked her arm around Lily's waist.

Leo and Owen pushed through the men, coming to stand beside him and guard the girls.

Coop stood at the edge of the melee. Blood dripped from his split lip.

He looked... Collin had never seen a look of such pure disgust from his brother before.

Coop mouthed something that Collin couldn't understand.

Collin didn't have time to soothe his brother's wounded feelings. This was about protecting Stella and her family.

"You want to tell me what's going on?"

Collin didn't know whether Leo's question was directed at him or Stella. When she stubbornly didn't answer, he opened his mouth.

Stella tensed beside him, as if afraid of what he would say.

Clarence Turnbull spat blood mixed with saliva on the ground. "I know what's been goin' on. They been lyin' to us this whole time." He pointed a finger at Collin. "And you're obviously mixed up in it too."

"They prob'ly been spying on us this whole time," called one man.

"Comin' up with ways to steal from us."

"We trusted 'em."

Collin wanted to defend Stella. She hadn't done anything but mind her own business.

But she had lied to everyone about her true identity. There was no denying it.

"Go back about your business," Owen said. "We'll leave it to Hollis to sort this out."

Clarence whirled on him. "When are you gonna get it through your skull that Hollis ain't comin' back?"

Owen stared him down. Clarence stepped back.

Then Owen motioned to Stella and Lily. "You'd better come with me."

FOURTEEN

"Why didn't you tell me?" Leo walked next to Collin, each step toward camp partially blocking Stella from his view. Coop was on Leo's other side, glaring at Collin.

Who was conscious of how Owen had inserted himself next to Stella. Stella and Lily had linked arms.

"It wasn't my secret to tell," he grumbled.

Owen was still acting captain. He had a duty to protect the two women.

But Collin still didn't like how the other men had surrounded them. He needed to be closer.

Leo seemed to read his mind, because he said, "Owen won't let anything happen to them."

But Owen was one man. And several of the men had been angry when Stella's hat had been knocked off.

"It's not fair to punish them," Collin said. "They've carried their own weight for the entire journey."

"How've they carried their own weight?" Coop argued. "Stephen—or whatever her name is—can't hunt a lick."

Collin held tightly to the last threads of his patience. Coop was frustrated at him. That much was certain from his twin's belligerent tone of voice. He'd claimed his hat back, scooping it up from the prairie ground.

Collin was frustrated right back.

"Neither can some of these other city men," Collin pointed out. "And no one's threatened to throw them out of the wagon train."

Maddie had come down from the wagon and now held onto the corner of the box, worry in the set of her shoulders. Had she seen the whole thing from there?

"Send Maddie over here," Owen told Clarence. "Don't lay a hand on her," he warned the other man. "And fetch Irene, too."

"Irene's sick," Stella said.

Someone jostled her from behind. Collin wanted to punch someone.

When they entered the circle of wagons, Alice and Evangeline looked up from where they were sitting next to the campfire.

Alice straightened, but Leo waved her off before she could come over.

Maddie joined Stella and Lily. Clarence followed a few paces behind. "The other un's real bad sick. Vomit all over her."

A couple of men murmured, but Owen didn't repeat his order to fetch her.

The three women stood in the center of the circled wagons.

Collin wanted to join them, stand beside Stella, but Leo held him back with a hand to his arm.

"Maddie's helped almost every family in this wagon train," Collin called out, loud enough for everyone to hear him. "She's put in stitches and made poultices and set broken bones."

"Doesn't change the fact that they lied to us," Clarence said. "Why're they playactin' they're menfolk? There's gotta be a reason."

"They're women traveling alone," Collin countered.

"So're Abigail and Felicity," Coop grumbled. His voice was low, but someone overheard.

Another man's voice rang out, "Yeah, what about those other two gals traveling' alone? No one's bothered them!"

Alice said something to Abigail, over near the fire.

"Hollis asked us to look after Abigail and Felicity," Leo said to Owen.

Abigail's head perked up.

"The Fairfaxes didn't have a Hollis to look out for them," Collin pointed out.

"Stay out of it," Leo said tightly.

Stella's chin came up. "I can speak for myself," she said sharply.

Maddie whispered something to her. Stella shook her head.

"C'mon," Leo said. "I want to talk to you."

"I'm not gonna walk away—"

Collin's protest was cut off as Leo and Coop crowded him, coming so close he had no choice but to take a step back.

Collin glanced at Stella, who was being interrogated by Owen. She didn't look in his direction.

Coop gave him a nudge that sent him another step away.

Collin hated this. Was this what Coop felt like when Collin and Leo tried to steer him out of trouble? Hot anger swirled inside, begging for a release.

"You don't know what she's been through," he said in a low, urgent voice.

Leo and Coop walked on either side of him. He imagined that if he tried to turn around, one of them would forcibly keep him walking with them.

"Did you even know?" Coop asked.

Yes.

"Or is this about her pretty face?" Coop went on. "Whatever she told you, she could've been lying to you."

He thought about Stella's independent streak that seemed a mile wide. About what she'd reluctantly told him, the words he'd almost had to pull out of her.

She wasn't lying. He was sure of it.

She didn't have an easy time trusting. And why should she?

He shook his head. "Stella's not like that."

"*Stella?*"

He couldn't understand why Coop was so all-fired upset about this. His brother seemed personally offended that Collin wanted to help Stella and her family.

"We should let Owen handle it," Leo said. "We've got enough trouble of our own."

He meant Evangeline's money. Collin lost his hold on his temper the tiniest bit. "A week ago, you wouldn't even call Owen your brother. Now you're willing to let him decide whether those girls stay in the wagon train or not?"

Leo's expression fell into a frown. "Keep your voice down."

They'd reached their wagon. Alice and Evangeline stood near the fire, wearing almost identical expressions of concern.

Abigail was tending to Felicity in the tent, her back visible through the open flaps.

"We can't risk you getting mixed up in the middle of—whatever that is." Leo gestured toward where Owen and the other men stood off against Stella and her sisters.

"Why not?" Collin asked sharply. "Because it doesn't fit into your plan, big brother?"

"Because if we get kicked out of the wagon train along with them, we'll be stranded at Fort Kearny. Do you know how dangerous that would be? We'd be vulnerable without the other wagons. Without a wagon master."

"I'm not just gonna leave her to the wolves," Collin said. If Stella and her family were abandoned out here, it'd be even worse for them.

"*Her*," Coop spat. "You hear that, big brother? It's all about the woman."

Collin lost his tenuous hold on his temper and whirled on his brother, shoving Coop's shoulder. "Shut up!"

Coop bounced back, giving Collin a shove of his own.

But Collin didn't back down. "I've been a part of cleaning up all of your messes," he hissed. "I've kept you out of jail, cleaned up after you drank yourself into a stupor. You think I wanted to do those things?"

Some of the fight went out of Coop. He rocked back on his heels, his stare wary.

"For once, try thinking about someone other than yourself." Collin meant the words for Coop, but he aimed them at both his brothers.

Collin stalked off, shaking. Not toward Stella but out into the darkness beyond the ring of wagons.

He hadn't meant to say those things to his twin.

He'd surprised himself. Because they were true. And the realization rocked him.

For the first time, he resented Coop.

"WHAT ARE WE GOING TO DO?" Maddie asked.

"I don't know," Stella returned.

She and Maddie sat on a pair of empty crates near their wagon. Neither of them—nor Lily, who'd disappeared inside the wagon—had the gumption to start the fire.

Owen had questioned her for a half hour while some of the men—like Collin and his brothers—had slipped away to their own wagons. The angry mob had dwindled, but it hadn't gone completely.

Four men seemed the most angry. Even now, Elroy Jenkins stood in front of his wagon with his arms crossed, staring at them. What did he expect she would do? Hold a gun on him and rob him now that her identity as a woman had been revealed?

What a mess.

Everything was unraveling around her.

Owen hadn't been cold, exactly, as he'd questioned her. More like detached. As if he had to hold himself distant before he decided her fate and that of her sisters.

She had told him only the bare basics. About landing in New York with high hopes, their belongings and money being stolen, deciding to come West, the men who'd chased them through the Chicago train station, Irene's certainty that she'd seen one of those men out here on the prairie.

She hadn't told him about the theft. She'd trusted Collin with that information, but not Owen. Collin had become... a friend.

She'd breathed not a word of the jeweled necklace around Irene's neck, either.

She hadn't meant to help Irene steal it. She hadn't known. She wanted no part of it, didn't know whether

Irene planned to sell it—to whom?—when they arrived in the Willamette Valley.

Had Irene only been using them to escape the Byrne brothers? Bringing her along had been a mistake.

It was the only conclusion Stella could come to. And now Irene was dangerously ill.

She was certain that if Owen or anyone on the wagon train found out about the jewel and how it'd been obtained, they *would* be thrown out of the wagon train. And then what?

They'd be easy targets. None of them was a good shot with a gun, even after Collin's lessons.

Lily emerged from the wagon, carefully stepping down using the spokes of the newly-replaced wagon wheel.

Except it was Lily as Stella hadn't seen her in weeks. She'd wasted no time in ditching the trousers. She'd donned a pretty, dark pink dress.

Their wagon was still parked where it'd been since it rolled up to camp last night; next to the Masons' wagon. The flickering light from their cook fire illuminated Lily's womanly figure, her hair down around her shoulders.

Coop did a double-take and said something low to Alice, who barely looked over before she returned to her meal.

Stella's stomach was gnawing with hunger, but it was Alice's indifference that truly made her gut twist.

Yesterday, when she'd been Stephen, Alice had welcomed her into camp. She'd been quick to offer to share the meal she'd prepared, and Stella had been... hopeful that maybe a friendship could bloom.

It'd happened with Collin, hadn't it?

But Collin had known.

And now Alice wouldn't even look in her direction.

"You two didn't want to start the fire?" Lily murmured the complaint as she pulled some kindling and two logs from the small pile stacked near the rear wagon wheel.

"We're trying to figure out what to do," Maddie said.

Except Stella's thoughts had been as scattered as some of the destroyed wagons they'd driven past yesterday.

"That's easy." Lily stacked the wood into a cone shape with the small pieces underneath the bigger ones. "Stella needs to cozy up to Collin and ask him to marry her."

Stella choked on the air she'd been breathing. She coughed, her eyes watering.

Too bad it didn't block out the sight of Maddie unsuccessfully trying to hide her smile.

"You like him, don't you?" Lily pressed.

A memory of his arm around her and the press of his mouth burst into Stella's mind. She flushed and only hoped her sisters wouldn't notice. She'd been trying to put the kiss out of her mind since it'd happened.

"We all saw it, when the two of you found us out in the woods," Maddie said.

Stella shook her head.

"He likes you, too," Lily added.

Stella couldn't help thinking of his tender touch, the way he'd looked at her just after their kiss. Like he wanted to kiss her again.

"Although he'd probably like you more if you'd go put on a dress." Under Lily's ministrations, tiny flames sparked. It would grow stronger.

"And wash your hair," Maddie said. "You need to brush that rat's nest out."

Stella shook her head. "I'm not changing clothes. How would I strap on a gun belt wearing a dress?" She pulled a face at Maddie. "And I'll mind my own hygiene, thank you."

Her sisters exchanged a speaking glance.

"She didn't say she wasn't going to propose to him," Lily pointed out.

"I'm not going to propose to him," Stella said.

Lily frowned.

Maddie did, too. "But you like him. And if you were hitched to one of the Spencers, you'd be under their protection."

"And so would we," Lily murmured.

It was a mercenary way of looking at marriage. And Stella could easily see a problem.

"Or," she said, "everyone could turn against Collin and kick him out of the wagon train along with us."

Lily scoffed. "They wouldn't do that. Everyone likes him."

"You've helped many families on this journey," Stella said. She stood and brushed off the seat of her pants. "Their goodwill didn't last long."

She'd tended Kyle Stewart's wife several days while she'd been sick. And he'd been one of the loudest voices calling for them to be kicked out of the wagon train.

"His older brother was captain," Lily argued. "He won't let Collin get kicked out."

"Maybe," Stella said. She stared into the crackling fire as Lily fed it sticks.

Her sisters turned to talking about what they could quickly prepare for a meal. Stella let their voices wash over her as her mind worked.

She and Maddie hadn't told Lily about the necklace. Their problems were bigger than just their identities being found out.

Stella needs to ask Collin to marry her.

There was a part of her that hadn't rejected the wild idea outright.

It was the same part of seventeen-year-old Stella, disguised as a young man, who never joined the circles of other boys on their lunch break at the factory. Never joined their camaraderie, never breached their friendship that was deeper than a surface "hello" in the mornings. She'd watched a group of three friends cover for a young man who was ill one day, helping with his tasks so he still got paid even though he was red-faced and feverish with shaking hands.

She'd never had that. She'd always stayed on the outskirts of the groups at the factory. Taken her lunch by herself.

She'd been afraid of being found out. Afraid of losing their families' income.

But she'd wanted to be included. Wanted to feel she had friends to lean on.

Her sisters had always been there for her. But they also looked up to her, trusted her to take care of them.

Who takes care of you? Collin's question from two days ago popped into her mind.

She thought of what it would be like to have Collin take care of her. He'd shielded her body with his when the tornado had come. Had helped her even when she'd been unkind to him.

What would it be like to be his wife?

Would he even want that?

He likes you.

So her sisters thought. But what did they know?

Even after they'd eaten a quick meal of pan biscuits and hardtack, and Lily and Maddie had drifted off in their bedrolls beneath the wagon, she stayed awake. Partly to keep watch, but partly because she couldn't stop thinking about their outlandish suggestion.

It would never work.

And she didn't dare ask.

Did she?

FIFTEEN

"We're pulling out in the morning, after the funeral." Leo said.

Rousted from his bedroll only moments before, it took a sleep-addled Collin a few moments to register their meaning.

He looked forward to the end of the journey, when he could expect a full night's sleep.

But with Evangeline sitting on a wagon full of bank notes, sleep wasn't going to happen anytime soon. Leo wanted one of their party on guard at all times.

It was nearing dawn, though the first rays of sunlight weren't showing yet.

Collin's jaw cracked with a yawn. He kept his voice low, conscious of the folks sleeping in tents and bedrolls around them. "What about Hollis?"

Last he'd seen before he'd turned in to bed, Leo and Owen had stood near the fire, with almost identical stances, each holding a cup of coffee as they'd talked.

"It's been three days," Leo said now. "August has been

tracking night and day. But..." He shook his head.

But no one had found Hollis.

"Who's gonna lead the wagon train?" he pressed.

He could see Leo's exhaustion in the way his shoulders had rounded. His brother's expression was only a shadow in the darkness.

"Owen wants to get us to the fort. There'll be another train or two passing through soon. Hopefully, we can join up with one of them."

That sounded risky. They'd paid Hollis to take them to Oregon. Was another wagon master really going to let them just join in the middle of the journey?

Or suppose they had to pay again? Collin knew that Leo and Evangeline had the money now—her inheritance from her father was in that wagon. But many of the families had scrimped and saved for years to afford Hollis's fee and their supplies.

"What about the Fairfaxes?" he asked.

Leo rubbed his hand down his face. "I don't know." His voice emerged muffled. When he lowered his hand, it was to put both hands on his hips. "Owen thinks they're still keeping secrets. He wanted to talk to you earlier, but you'd gone off alone."

"I only know the basics. Same as what she told him."

But he'd sensed she was holding something back that morning, hadn't he?

"She's just trying to take care of her family. Like you've done all these years. You're a good brother."

Stella and Leo were more alike than they knew.

But Collin's compliment had Leo sizing him up, not what Collin had intended. "Maybe Coop's right. Maybe you're too close to the situation to see straight."

"I see just fine," Collin said. He meant to mash his hat

on his head, but he still didn't have one, not after giving his to Stella and it being blown away in the storm. He ran his hand through his hair instead. "I'll take my turn on watch."

He dismissed himself and heard Leo's soft sigh as he walked out of the ring of wagons.

Collin held his rifle in one hand, every shadow a threat as his eyes adjusted to the dark.

He was the one seeing straight. Stella and her family needed help.

And after all the times he'd taken care of Coop's messes, all the times he'd come at Leo's beck and call, his brothers didn't trust his judgment. And wouldn't lend him their support.

It stung.

His feet turned toward Stella's wagon without a conscious thought. If he knew her at all, he knew she wasn't sleeping.

He needed to talk to her. Just being in her presence made him feel settled. And he needed that right now, when everything felt so jumbled and upside down.

He was still several yards from her wagon when something moved at the front of the conveyance.

He stopped walking. "It's me," he whispered.

A shadow separated from the darker silhouette of the wagon. Stella. Moving toward him.

He wasn't prepared for her to throw herself against him. He fell back a step but then balanced and caught her against him with an arm around her waist. Her arms went around his neck and, for a moment, she pressed close in his embrace.

His empty hand came into her hair, still loose down her back. The softness of it and the feel of her in his arms undid him.

"We need to talk," he whispered. He couldn't help himself. His jaw was already brushing hers. He pressed a kiss against her cheek.

She stretched up and brushed a kiss to his chin. "So talk," she whispered.

He couldn't navigate through the muddle of his thoughts, not with her in his arms like this. She felt *right*. A perfect fit.

Like she was his.

So he did what felt like the most natural thing to do and lowered his mouth to kiss hers.

In the dark, it wouldn't have worked if they hadn't been thinking the same thing, if she didn't lift her mouth to meet his. He would've kissed the crown of her head or gotten an elbow in his eye.

But she met him sweetly, her lips soft and cool. She was trembling. Or maybe that was him, the force of the emotions sweeping through him.

He cared about her. Deeply.

Which was why he didn't want to make things worse for her. He didn't want her reputation to be tarnished, didn't want anyone in camp to have more reason to distrust her.

He eased back, heart still racing from the kiss, the feel of her in his arms.

He touched her jaw, brushed her cheek with his thumb. "You all right?"

She shook her head slightly. *No.*

"Come with me?" he breathed the question. "We can talk more freely a little farther from camp."

He took her hand and led her several more yards out into the darkness. Here, the wagons and tents were barely visible.

Hopefully, they would be, too, if anyone was looking.

"Leo just told me everyone is planning to move on tomorrow," he said, still whispering. "Head to the fort and see if we can join up with another wagon train coming through."

Still holding her hand, he felt the fine tension in her.

"What about us?"

"I don't know. Leo wouldn't tell me what Owen decided."

She shuddered. He let go of her hand to rub both her arms.

Her hands rested on his chest. "Collin, I—"

He liked being close like this. She was barely leaning on him, but her nearness made him want to protect her.

"I want to help," he said. "But I don't know how to make them listen to me."

"Maddie and Lily said—they think we should get married."

For a breathless moment, the thought swirled through him, lighting him up like the lightning that had flashed through the sky during the storm.

"But it's a ridiculous idea," she added

He crashed back to earth like a boom of thunder.

STELLA DIDN'T KNOW what had possessed her to utter the outlandish words. What was she thinking?

Maddie and Lily think we should get married.

Collin's hands dropped away from her arms, and her hands fell to her sides. It had become light enough that she was suddenly aware of the empty space between them.

"You'd better start over. What did your sisters say?"

She didn't know if she could say it again. Her face was burning already.

"Your family has good standing with Hollis and the wagon train." Everyone looked up to Leo, even though some of the men had been desperate and the company was unruly right now.

"If... if we got married, Maddie and Lily and I would be connected to your family. We'd have your protection. Maybe...maybe the other men would let us stay."

It sounded so mercenary. What must he think?

She admired him. Deeply. She *liked* him.

But those words stuck behind her throat. She'd spent so long being the protector, keeping her emotions hidden to protect herself that she was too afraid to voice them.

The first silver rays of light poked over the horizon. They wouldn't have long before the camp woke up and people would begin milling about.

Collin looked to the side, a muscle jumping in his jaw. "You've come this far on your own strength and wits."

"I have to think of Lily and Maddie." Getting them to Oregon, starting a new life, a *safe* life was the most important thing.

He stared at her now, with his back to the rising sun. His face was in shadow. "So this would be out of convenience only. Nothing more."

The words were right there, clogging her throat, but she couldn't get them out. The part of her that wanted to belong to someone whispered that if she was forced into this marriage, it would be all right because it was *Collin*.

But she swallowed them back. It was too much of a risk to let him in.

"Yes." The word stuck in her throat, and she had to clear it. "That's all it would be."

He was quiet then.

The sun emerged over the horizon. She could see the smoky outline of his breath in the cool air.

Why didn't he say anything?

Her face burned hotter and hotter. Lily and Maddie had been so sure that he liked her.

She'd thought that's what his kisses meant, too.

"I'm flattered," he said finally. "But I'm not sure that's the kind of marriage I want. One made out of desperation."

She heard the words he didn't say. *I'm not sure I want to marry you.*

Humiliation rolled over her in a wave as big as the gusts of wind that had nearly knocked her from her horse before. She lowered her gaze.

"I understand." Her thoughts spun. She'd dismissed the girls' plan at first, but as the night had worn on, she'd latched on to it as their best hope.

She hadn't considered that he might say no.

She felt breathless, anxious feelings tightening like a cinch around her chest. What were they going to do? What if the company decided to leave them behind?

"Stella." He repeated her name, exasperation in his voice. So different from the husky whisper he'd used when he'd embraced her not long ago. "I'm not saying no."

He wasn't?

"I need to think about it."

Her heart was pounding. She was a mess of confusion and hurt and hope and anxiety.

"I need to get back to the wagon," she murmured.

She felt his eyes on her, but she couldn't quite meet his gaze.

"I'll catch up with you later," he called after her.

Maddie and Lily were already awake when she

reached the wagon. So were their neighbors and folks all around the camp.

Since Maddie and Lily didn't know what she'd gone and done, they didn't ask. And she kept her trap shut. She felt trembly and uncertain. Not the Stella who'd been filled with bravado and confidence that this journey was the answer, that they could make it.

What were they going to do?

Irene was worse this morning. She couldn't keep down the water that Maddie spoon-fed her. Maddie's expression was grave when she climbed down from the wagon.

"The Welborns' have a milk cow," Maddie murmured. "But I doubt they'd give us even a half cup of milk now."

The camp was somber as everyone packed up the wagons.

And the mood grew even more serious as they gathered at the edge of the circle to remember those who'd passed away in the storm. Stella's eyes kept bouncing to the bodies wrapped in quilts and blankets and then away.

Owen was speaking, but she and her sisters were at the back of the group and her mind couldn't seem to focus on his words. Collin and his family were on the far side of the crowd.

She was the first one to notice the man leading a horse appearing over the horizon. He walked straight toward them.

August Mason. Why wasn't he riding?

She saw the bundle tied to his saddle and nudged Maddie, then tipped her chin.

Maddie followed her gaze.

Was that...?

"Hollis," Maddie whispered.

Was he dead? Was August bringing them another body to bury?

Someone called out from farther up in the crowd, and Owen stopped what he was saying. He joined two other men as they went to meet August.

Maddie started to move, as if she wanted to join them, but Stella held her arm. People were suspicious of them now. She wanted her sister close, just in case.

"He's alive," one of the men called back.

Owen was already doubling back. He came to Stella and her sisters like an arrow shot straight.

"He's unconscious. Has an injury to his head. Can you nurse him?" he directed the words to Maddie.

"Of—" Maddie had already started to answer before Stella squeezed her arm.

"If we help him, we stay," Stella said quickly.

Lily remained silent and watchful.

Owen's eyes glittered. Maybe it was even more mercenary than her proposal to Collin.

Owen might even guess she was bluffing. She wouldn't keep Maddie from helping Hollis, even if Owen said no. But she had to try.

"It'll be Hollis's decision," Owen said.

"If he lives," she returned. "If Maddie helps him, I want him to know just who it was that saved his life."

She didn't even know if Maddie could do it.

Finally, Owen nodded.

Collin met her gaze from several feet away. He must've heard everything.

She'd been too hasty with her proposal. She'd embarrassed them both.

Good thing he hadn't said yes.

SIXTEEN

Collin woke from a deep sleep, a rough hand shaking his shoulder.

He blinked bleary eyes open, registering his bedroll and the person hovering over him.

Coop.

"What'sa matter?" he mumbled, batting his brother's hand away.

"The cattle are gone. I need your help."

He shook his head to clear it, sitting up in his bedroll. Had he heard Coop right?

It was close to dawn the next day, the eastern horizon turning gray. Coop was already several steps away. Collin quickly pushed out of his bedroll. He shook out his boots to make sure there were no critters inside and stuffed his feet in them.

"Where's Leo?" Collin asked when he'd caught up to his twin.

"Sleeping."

Collin trailed his brother past the wagon and out into

the open prairie beyond. The horses were ground-tied, as usual.

But the cattle were gone. Twenty-eight head, and not a one of them in sight.

Coop's horse was already saddled. He strode to Collin's gelding and hefted the saddle onto its back.

"What happened?" Collin stared at the churned up ground where the cattle had been sleeping during his watch in the middle of the night. The company had decided to stay put once Hollis had been found, gravely injured. Everyone seemed anxious to have their wagon master back.

Coop had been on watch after Collin. How had the cattle disappeared?

"I fell asleep," Coop said. "Been one too many nights on watch…"

His twin was lying.

The sun was up enough for Collin to see the way his brother's right hand twitched at his side, the slightest squint to his eyes.

Coop kept buckling the saddle. "Something must've spooked 'em. I came to when I heard a rumbling of hooves, but by the time I… ah, woke up all the way, they were running off. We gotta catch up to them."

"Wait a minute." Collin rubbed one hand down his face. Was he still dreaming? He couldn't quite get his thoughts to line up. "We need to wake Leo," he said.

Coop scowled.

"If you don't know what scared them, it coulda been anything. An animal. Or some men looking for trouble. We can't just ride into it."

Coop pointed to the rifle in its leather scabbard, attached to his saddle. "That's what our guns are for."

Collin started back toward Leo and Evangeline's tent. "I'm gonna wake him. At least tell him we're going after them."

Leo had enough to worry about with his new family and protecting what was theirs. If he woke to find the twins gone and the cattle gone, he'd have a conniption.

Coop caught up to him in two jogged strides. He grabbed Collin's arm. "Tell him we switched watches."

Collin stopped walking, staring at his twin. Coop's expression was hard, his eyes closed off.

"Why would I do that?" Collin asked. "Leo woke me for second watch. He knows I was there."

"Tell him you took my watch too. That I wanted the extra sleep."

"Why? What're you trying to hide?" Collin demanded.

"Nothin'." But there was that squint again.

"Stop lying." Collin's temper sparked. He wanted to shove his brother. Or maybe punch him. Take him by the shoulders and shake him until some sense rolled into his head.

Coop's expression didn't change. "Leo's already barely talking to me. This wasn't my fault."

How many times had Collin heard that over the years? His brother had taken advantage of Collin's love for him and let Collin take the blame numerous times.

But this was one time too many.

Maybe he would've felt different if his brother had backed him up when things had gone down with Stella yesterday. But Coop hadn't stood by him, hadn't supported him.

And now he wanted Collin to lie for him?

They'd already wasted precious minutes, and the sun was up.

Leo's head appeared above the tent. He looked rumpled in the morning light. Happy, his face clear of the weight of duty he usually carried.

And then he turned and caught sight of Collin and Coop, and his expression shuttered.

Collin waved him over, urgency in the movements.

Owen straightened up from where he'd been kneeling over the ashes from last night's fire, stacking twigs. Collin hadn't seen him there. He trailed Leo, joining them.

Coop went tense behind Collin.

"What's going on?" Leo asked. He glanced behind them and saw for himself. "Where are the cattle?"

"Gone," said Coop. "Something spooked 'em."

"How?" Leo demanded.

"Who was on watch?" Owen asked, his words trailing after Leo's so that his question hung in the air.

Collin knew Coop was waiting for him to answer. To lie. To take Leo's disappointment on his behalf.

"Coop was," Collin said. The words tasted bitter in his mouth somehow. "He claims he fell asleep. The two of us are going after them."

Leo and Owen exchanged a glance. Something about it hit Collin hard. He and Coop used to be able to read each others' thoughts with a glance. Not in a long time, though.

"I'll go myself," Coop said bitterly. "I see how things are now. You care more about a pretty face than your brother."

"You know that's not true," Collin said.

Coop was already shaking his head, walking toward his horse.

"Coop!" Leo called out, but Coop pulled his hat low over his eyes and didn't look back. "Be careful," Leo warned Collin.

"You want me to go along?" Owen asked.

Collin was the one who shook his head now. "Watch out for Stella. And her family."

Collin hadn't had a chance to talk to her since yesterday morning.

Maddie and Lily think we should get married.

He still couldn't believe she'd asked it of him. He'd wanted to say yes. Until it became apparent that she wasn't doing it because she had feelings for him. She would marry him for her sisters.

He wanted more. He wanted her heart.

He jogged after Coop, looking back once to see Leo and Owen conversing, frowns on their faces.

Coop's expression was like a thundercloud as he stepped up into the saddle. "I said I'd fetch them myself."

He sounded angry.

But Collin was angry too. What right did Coop have to ask Collin to cover for him?

Coop rode his horse right into Collin's path, drawing him up short. "Go back and be with your woman, why don't you?"

It was Collin's turn to scowl. "She's not my woman. And maybe I'm done taking the blame for you, but that doesn't mean you're not my brother. I'm gonna help you, you stubborn coot."

Coop's angry expression intensified. "I never asked you to take blame for me. Not if it meant this."

They weren't talking about the cattle any more. They both knew it.

This was about New Jersey.

Coop hadn't asked, because he'd been drunk as a skunk that night.

And that was as good as the same thing, in Collin's books.

Collin held his gaze. "Yes, you did."

The moment stretched between them, fraught with tension. For a moment, Collin thought his brother might run him over with the horse.

Finally, Coop rode off in a gallop, leaving Collin choking on dust in his wake.

He went for his own horse. Things might be broken between them. Maybe even beyond repair.

But he wasn't letting his brother ride out alone.

IT WAS MID MORNING, and Stella hadn't seen Collin once today.

They'd been pulled separate directions yesterday. She'd seen the tension between him and his family, and even though she'd wanted to finish the conversation between them, she'd been afraid to make things worse for him.

Was he avoiding her now?

She was conscious of Alice and Evangeline in camp, only a few yards away. Abigail had been there earlier. Stella had watched her help her friend, Felicity, hobble away from camp. Felicity had been gravely injured, and the Spencers had taken her and Abigail in. Probably she wanted some privacy to wash up.

Alice and Evangeline worked like friends, giggling when tiny Sara climbed on top of a crate and then hopped off.

Sara tilted her head, watching them in their giggles.

And then promptly did it again.

Even Stella was tempted to smile. Until Alice glanced in her direction and caught her watching. She quickly went back to scrubbing out the cookpot from the remains of breakfast.

Maddie emerged from the third tent in the Spencers' camp. The one where she'd been doctoring Hollis since yesterday. He'd come to just after dark, to the relief of everyone in camp. But he hadn't been able to stay awake long.

When Maddie had finally slipped into her bedroll, she'd been visibly worried.

And now she looked exasperated.

"The stubborn man wants to wash up," she told Alice, loud enough that Stella could hear. "He can barely hold his head up off the pillow, but he wants to wash."

Alice grinned. "I've got some experience with stubborn men."

Evangeline said something too low for Stella to hear.

Maddie glanced in Stella's direction, saw her eaves-dropping. "Stella will fetch water from the creek. Won't you?" she called out.

Stella nodded and picked up a couple of pails she'd already been using to tote water.

She hurried away before Alice could say she didn't want Stella's help. She was back soon enough, her pant legs wet where she'd spilled some of the water in her hurry.

"Thanks," Alice said when Stella put the pails at the edge of the fire. Evangeline and Sara were gone now.

Stella stood awkwardly, then wiped her hands on her pant legs. "I'm—sorry. For pretending."

She hadn't made an apology to anyone else. Alice considered her. Didn't say anything.

The moment grew awkward.

"I can bring more water, if you need it," Stella said.

What she really wanted was a chance to make friends with Alice. She wasn't good at this sort of thing, though.

"We could use more wood for the fire," Alice said, looking down.

Maddie had been at the Fairfaxes' wagon mixing up a poultice, but now she approached.

"Did August say anything else about how he'd found Hollis?" Maddie asked Alice.

"Not much." Alice prodded the pails closer to the fire so they would heat.

"His wound..." Maddie trailed off. "It seems like he was struck from behind."

Alice winced. Was she squeamish?

"If he got caught by the twister, he could've been thrown into something," Stella pointed out. "The wind was so powerful..."

Maddie's gaze had gone far-off, like she was thinking. "But August said he'd found Hollis in a hollow, as if he were trying to climb up the hill to get out of it."

It'd been days before he'd been found. And his horse was missing, had never been found. If he'd had such a bad head injury, he might've gotten turned around. There was no telling how he'd ended up where he had.

"Maybe now he'll be able to tell us what happened," Alice said.

Maddie frowned. "I tried asking him, moments ago. He seems disoriented. Didn't know how he'd gotten back to camp. I didn't want to push. He needs to rest. Head wounds can be tricky."

"What's that mean?" Alice asked.

"It means he shouldn't overdo it. He might need to rest

for several days. Even a week. He'll have headaches. Maybe get dizzy or have trouble balancing enough to walk."

Alice winced. "Doesn't sound like he's going to be happy for the next little while."

Maddie shook her head.

Everyone knew the wagon master's independence and self-reliance. He wasn't going to like being coddled, even if it was for his own good.

Maddie moved back toward the tent again. "I'll tell him his wash water is heating up. If he's still awake."

Her sister leaving meant she didn't have a reason to stay, not when Alice had asked for her help with firewood.

She excused herself.

Wood was scarce underneath the trees that ran alongside the winding creek. They'd been in this camp for days. Longer than they'd been anywhere else. Everyone had been searching for wood in the same places.

Stella wandered farther. This wasn't the most ideal task. It gave her mind too much time to think.

She was still embarrassed about what she asked of Collin. She treasured their friendship, forged in this wilderness. She didn't want anything to change between them. She knew Collin's brother had taken advantage of his good nature and compassion in the past. What if he thought she was trying to do the same thing?

She didn't have an answer, and when she arrived back at camp, she noticed that the cattle that the Spencers had been herding we're gone. Collin was still gone too.

Alice gave her a quick thank you for the wood as she was toting water towards Hollis's tent.

Stella went back to her own wagon. She could hear Lily and Irene inside. But Maddie was nowhere to be seen.

Stella knocked on the wagon box. "Lily, do you know where Maddie went?"

"She went to check on the Kimballs."

Mrs. Kimball was expecting her third baby and had been having indigestion for several days.

But Stella had a clear view of the woman across camp. She sat on a crate near her own campfire, her hand resting on her belly. Maddie was nowhere in sight.

Unease twisted her gut.

She waited a few moments, but Maddie didn't reappear. So Stella went over to speak to Mrs. Kimball.

"I'm sorry to bother you," she started politely.

The woman frowned, her eyes skittering away. Stella remembered that her husband had been one of the most vocal when her identity had been revealed.

"Have you seen my sister, Maddie?"

There was a disdainful curl to the woman's lips, but she answered, "She was talkin' to somebody. I dunno who."

"She didn't wanna go with him!" A five-year-old boy piped up. He'd been sitting at Mrs. Kimball's feet, scratching in the dirt with a stick.

Stella's heart flipped. Who had Maddie been talking to?

"Did you see her?" she asked the boy.

He nodded, his eyes still on the ground. "He grabbed her arm 'n dragged her away."

"Hush now," Mrs. Kimball said sharply. Her lips pinched. "We don't tell stories."

Now he looked up, eyes flashing and chin jutting out. "It ain't a story. I saw him take her."

Stella's heart pounded furiously. "Please—" Her voice cracked, and she had to start over. "If my sister's in trouble..."

She didn't know what she would do. She glanced around. Everything in camp seemed so normal. A man two wagons over was skinning a rabbit. Children chattered from a wagon past him.

How could no one else have noticed Maddie being dragged away?

She squatted to the boy's level. "Did you see which way they went?"

He stared her square in the face, then lifted his arm and pointed south.

Stella's chest felt locked and tight as she ran through the center of the circled wagons. Her hands shook as she attempted to saddle the stallion. A glance at the Spencers' campsite showed only Alice. No men. No Collin.

Lily jumped off the wagon and reached Stella as she was tightening the cinch. "What's the matter?" she asked.

"Maddie's gone. I think someone took her." Stella hated the way her voice shook.

"Wait—"

But Stella didn't wait. She stepped into the saddle.

Lily looked frantic, high color in her cheeks. "You can't go after her alone. You need help."

Stella kept her eyes averted from Collin's camp. "Who's going to help me?" she asked with a bitter twist to her lips. No one. That was the answer to who would help them. "You saw the way the men reacted to us yesterday."

"But what about—"

She couldn't wait for Lily to wrap her head around it.

"Stay in camp," she ordered her sister.

And she rode off. Alone.

SEVENTEEN

I t took half the day to round up the scattered cattle.

Coop didn't say one word during all that time. He barely looked in Collin's direction.

Collin was wearing what felt like an inch of dust that the cattle had kicked up, and he was starving. He'd missed breakfast and lunch and his saddlebag had been empty of anything that would fill his stomach.

Leo must have been watching for them because he rode out to meet them.

Coop was on the western-most side of the herd; Collin was on the eastern-most. Leo veered toward Collin, but waved Coop over to meet them.

There was a resentful part of Collin that wanted Leo to lecture Coop for falling down on his responsibility.

Instead, Leo said, "After the two of you left, Owen and I noticed some footprints between the wagons and where the cattle were last night."

Collin's brows drew together. What?

"There's footprints all over," Coop said. "We've been camped here for days."

"These were fresh. We think somebody scared the cattle away."

And Coop hadn't been doing his job on watch, because they'd gotten away with it.

Coop evidently didn't miss the subtext. Color rose in his neck.

"Why would someone want to spook our cattle?" Collin asked.

Coop shot him a glare. Collin ignored his twin.

Leo shook his head. "I don't know yet. But we've got to be more vigilant."

Coop's jaw locked.

"I need to talk to Coop," Leo said.

Collin nodded and went in search of his lunch.

He dismounted from his horse and left the animal to graze for a bit. He drew up short outside of the ring of wagons. There... in a muddy place without much grass. The footprints Leo had been talking about. A lot of them. Like someone had been watching for quite a while.

Be more vigilant.

Leo was already spread thin between making sure the family wagon and the cattle were all right, as well as taking care of his new wife and her younger sister.

Did that mean more responsibility would fall on Coop?

His brain was a little fuzzy from lack of food. And he didn't want to think about Coop any more.

He walked into their campsite, but the area was curiously empty. Two tents were open. Collin could see Felicity in one, Hollis in the other. The wagon master appeared to be sleeping or unconscious. Felicity was awake, her gaze jumping to him and then away, as if he wasn't interesting enough to hold her attention.

He'd seen the way her eyes followed August around camp. Kind of hard not to notice.

An angel he suspected was named Alice had left two plates covered in checked towels on the tailgate.

He was glad their campsite was empty. It meant there was no one around to see him tear into the venison steak and pan biscuit as if he was a ravenous animal.

He'd only finished half, his belly was still grumbling for sustenance, when he saw Lily Fairfax hurrying in his direction.

She'd been wearing a dress since almost the moment they'd been found out, while Stella had kept to her trousers. Did Stella think it made her look tougher? More unapproachable?

It might've, if he hadn't gotten to know her.

Lily looked frightened as she made a beeline straight toward him. Collin's gaze flicked to her wagon. No one else was in sight. Where were Stella? Maddie? Irene?

"I need your help," Lily said in a rush. "Maddie disappeared, and Stella's gone after her, but—"

She was talking so fast her words were running together, and it was hard for him to follow.

"Slow down," he said. "What happened to Maddie?"

"One minute, she was in camp. Nursing Hollis and checking on Mrs. Kimball. And then she was.... gone. Stella asked after her, and said someone saw her get grabbed."

The food he'd just eaten felt like a rock in his stomach. "When?"

"Hours ago." Lily's voice shook. He set down his plate of food to put a brotherly hand on her shoulder.

"Stella rode off on the stallion. To find Maddie." A tear

slipped from Lily's eye, and she brushed it away impatiently.

He glanced over his shoulder. Where was Leo? He needed his brother, right now. "Who went with her?"

"No one."

His gaze whipped back to Lily. "What?"

She struggled to hold her tears back now. "I asked her not to go off alone, but she didn't listen. She said no one else would help."

He took a sweeping look around, one that encompassed the wide-open prairie beyond the campsite.

"Please," she said in a choked voice, "you have to find them."

"This the same fella who was after you at the train station?" He hadn't truly believed the threat was real. It had seemed so far-fetched...

She looked momentarily surprised that he knew about that. "I don't know. It has to be."

That sparked an idea.

"Let's talk to Irene for a minute," he said, already striding toward the Fairfax wagon. "Stella said Irene knew who was chasing you girls. Maybe she can tell me something that will help."

Lily led the way to their wagon at a dead run.

Irene was flushed with fever and wouldn't wake up, even when Lily shook her shoulder.

"She's worse than she was earlier," Lily said, obviously trying to hold off tears. "I don't know what to do. Maddie would know what to do."

He squeezed her shoulder. "I'll find her. Stella, too."

But he had no idea where to look.

He was backing away from the wagon when something

caught his eye. He leaned in closer. Tugged the chain from Irene's neck.

A huge, glittering red stone set in the middle of what looked like diamonds slipped free.

He glanced at Lily to find the young woman wearing a shocked expression filled with enough terror that he knew it was genuine.

"You didn't know?" he asked.

She shook her head.

He pulled the cord to close the canvas, then quickly stepped away from the wagon, holding Lily by the arm.

A rock like that had to be worth a lot. Maybe even more than Evangeline's bank notes.

He'd thought it didn't make sense for someone to be chasing the women out into the wilderness. But someone chasing a valuable jewel?

That *did* make sense.

"Did Stella know?" he demanded.

"I don't—I don't know," she stammered.

Had she been lying to him this whole time?

He didn't know what to think. He knew she was willing to do just about anything to protect her sisters. But he'd thought they'd had something special between them.

Had any of it been real?

He shook his head. These thoughts weren't helping right now.

He couldn't ask Leo to help him track Stella down, not when Leo needed all eyes on the cattle.

Lily said Maddie'd been taken by a single man. One man.

Collin would go alone. And hopefully intercept Stella on the way.

STELLA WENT in the direction the little boy had pointed. She'd raced off on the stallion's back with no regard for her own safety, barely feeling for the revolver at her hip.

She had no plan.

Only a terrible urgency to reach her sister. To make sure Maddie was safe.

She might not be the best tracker, but she'd picked up some skill by listening when the men had been on hunts. She'd been smart enough to stick close to August Mason, and when he got off his horse to examine the ground, she'd waited until he'd gone and then she did the same.

She'd learned that the two almost-teardrop shaped hooves close together meant a deer. She'd seen a small track like that of a dog and decided it must be a fox or maybe a coyote.

What she needed to track today was much larger. Horse hoof prints or men's footprints shouldn't be hard to find.

But they'd been camped in this area for days. Folks had hunted for firewood and game, and they'd been searching for survivors too. There were tracks everywhere.

She grew more panicky as the day wore on. She saw no sign of anyone.

She'd been so sure that no one would help her, but maybe she should have waited on Collin.

She didn't know anymore.

She must've traveled two or three miles from camp now. The prairie had slowly grown up into a wooded area that stretched as far as the eye could see. A large gully angled down, and now there were no longer prairie grasses beneath the horse's hooves, only a carpet of decaying leaves that muffled each hoofbeat.

And still no tracks. No sign that anyone had come this way.

A brisk breeze blew strands of her hair out of her braid and across her cheek. She reined in the stallion, trying to think what she should do next.

A nearby bush rattled. The stallion neighed and side-stepped.

Not now.

"Maddie!" She yelled out of desperation.

Nothing.

The wind pushed against her again. Clouds scuttled across the sky overhead.

That bush rattled.

The stallion bobbed his head.

He didn't like it here? Fine. Neither did she.

She squeezed her legs and used the reins to guide him into a turn.

He shook his head, prancing a few steps to the left. Toward that confounded bush.

"I need you—to obey me!" Her voice came out choked.

What was she even doing, talking to a horse?

He couldn't understand her.

In a moment of urgency and desperation, she kicked her feet against his middle.

And that set him off.

He whinnied and jolted. She grabbed for the saddle horn. What she'd thought was him jumping into a gallop wasn't it at all. He reared, and it was so unexpected that she lost her seat and tumbled from the saddle.

She shrieked, a kaleidoscope of colors whirring past her eyes as she fell. At least the ground would be soft—

Everything went black.

She came to moments later. Or maybe it had been longer than that.

She squinted up at the sky. The sun's bright rays shot arrows of pain through her skull. She reached up with one hand and touched her temple. Her fingers came away smeared with blood.

What—?

She pressed her hand against her throbbing head and felt along the ground with the other one. There was an exposed tree root, almost completely covered with fallen leaves from last autumn. She must've hit her head on it when she fell.

Maddie.

The stallion.

Where—?

She pushed through the pain and swiveled her head. The stallion was nowhere in sight.

No!

This couldn't be happening.

She put a trembling hand on the tree next to her and leaned heavily against it as she struggled to her feet. Why was she so shaky?

She'd be able to see better when she was standing. Surely the stallion was waiting for her down in the gully. Or maybe at the tree line, back the way they'd come.

But he wasn't anywhere to be seen. Fear choked her, knotted her stomach.

She was suddenly all turned around. Not sure which direction would take her back to camp—back to help.

Was there help for her there? Since her true identity had been revealed, she'd received only suspicion and anger.

Tears slipped down her face. She needed the stallion. It

would take twice as long to reach camp without him—if she could even get her bearings.

She leaned her shoulder against the tree. Her head hurt. It was too heavy. She leaned it against the rough bark of the tree.

She didn't know what to do.

But she knew she wanted Collin.

Collin had been a steady presence, a stone that wouldn't be moved even in the face of the tornado they'd weathered. He'd shielded her, protected her.

He'd seen her true self, the parts of her she was afraid to show anyone else, even her sisters.

And he hadn't turned away from her.

She'd botched that awful proposal. She had tried to explain logically the reasons they should get married.

When she should've told him how she truly felt.

She was falling in love with him. She hadn't meant for it to happen. It was inconvenient, and messy, and there was still danger and sisters and *Irene* to deal with.

But she wanted him by her side through all of it. She didn't need him to rescue her—though that would be nice right about now. She needed his steady support.

Would she even have a chance to tell him her realization? Her feelings?

She caught movement, but it was far off. A dark shadow moving along the far edge of the gully. The dappled sunlight filtering through the woods made it hard to see.

It could be a rogue cow—no. It was the stallion.

Too distant for her to catch him on foot.

She tried to whistle. Not only was the sound pitiful, more spit than sound, but the effort cost her dearly. Her head pounded worse.

She needed the horse. Maddie was in danger. It'd been too long. What if the Byrnes' man had hurt her?

Stella pushed away from the tree and took a painful step down the incline. On horseback, it hadn't seemed steep. Just a gentle slope down, among all the trees.

On foot, every step was fraught with peril.

A tree root she could trip on.

The half-rotted leaves beneath her feet slippery under her boots.

She misjudged her next step, the fallen leaves hiding a hole in the ground. Her ankle twisted. She went down with a cry.

More tears came.

She had to keep her eye on the stallion. Where—?

He'd moved farther away.

"No! Come back!"

She knew it was useless to call him.

But she couldn't give up. Maddie's life hung in the balance.

EIGHTEEN

The afternoon lengthened, and Stella grew more and more desperate

It was as if she had gone back to the very first day of this journey.

Her sisters were depending on her. And she had no one.

With a throbbing head and a foot that felt more tender with each step, she'd given up on trailing the stallion. She'd turned around, determined to make it back to camp on her own steam.

Mad-die. Mad-die. Mad-die.

The cadence of her steps was like a silent scream of her sister's name.

If something happened to Maddie, she would never forgive herself.

The realization came over her slowly.

She hadn't been able to understand why Collin had taken Coop's punishments, why he'd let his brother take advantage of him for years.

But they were the same, weren't they? If something happened to Coop, *Collin* would never forgive himself.

Oh, Collin.

She heard hoofbeats behind her and whirled, hand going automatically to the weapon at her hip.

It was the stallion. Sometime in the past moments, while she'd been lost in her thoughts, he'd begun following her.

Maybe for a while, because now he was only a handful of yards away.

Something shifted inside her, the hope that had been withering breathed back to life.

She turned back to face the direction she'd been going. And kept walking.

When she'd chased after the stallion, he ran away.

He's frightened.

That was Collin's voice, a reminder of that first night, when he'd gone to sleep on the banks of that creek and left her to try to catch the stallion on her own.

The stallion had been frightened again today by the odd sound from the bush. In her desperation to get to Maddie, she hadn't listened to the horse.

It's a partnership.

Collin had believed she could develop a relationship with the horse. She'd been too afraid of what would happen if she failed.

She hadn't even given him a name.

She didn't have many options. No candy in her pockets, no way to lure the horse.

But she could give him a name.

"What should we call you?" she asked softly. "You're a fine one. So big and strong. Maybe Prince? Or Galileo?"

Saying the silly name aloud made her smile, even amidst her worry.

When she glanced over her shoulder, the stallion had gained on her a little more.

"No, those aren't quite right. Hmm..."

She thought of Collin. Of the way he'd made her feel when he'd held her in his arms. The security, the feeling of peace.

No one else made her feel like that.

"Duncan," she said. The name was pulled from her most distant memories. Father had once mentioned a great-great-uncle by that name. He'd told her it meant "brown warrior."

The stallion was more black than brown, but the name seemed to fit.

She slowed to a stop and turned to face the stallion, who came two more steps and then stopped. He was roughly four yards away from her. Too far for her to leap and catch the reins that dragged the ground. He'd bolt if she tried that.

Think about Collin. She needed to remember his gentle way with the animal. His quiet confidence.

She felt anything but confident, but she asked, "Are you Duncan?"

The horse watched her. She forced herself to relax her hands, her shoulders, the muscles in her face.

"Duncan. I think that's your name. D'you like it?"

He whickered softly. His front hoof lifted, and for one moment she thought he would bolt.

And then he stepped toward her.

And then he did it again.

"Good boy. That's it, Duncan."

When he came close enough, she didn't try to grab for the reins. She lifted her hand, palm facing up to the sky.

He sniffed her, his breaths tickling her skin. He let her scratch beneath his chin. Let her rub both hands along the sides of his face.

He nudged her stomach with his nose.

Tears pricked her eyes. He'd come back to her. To help her.

Duncan was truly her horse.

"Let's go find Maddie," she whispered.

Duncan stood patiently while she checked the bridle and saddle. Her head *whooshed* and pounded when she climbed into the saddle.

But worry for Maddie spurred her on. She was going to find her sister. And she was going to rescue her.

She'd seen nothing this direction and feared that the little boy who'd pointed to the south had been wrong.

She headed back the way she'd come, starting a long climb out of the gully.

She was only halfway to the last line of trees when she caught movement from the corner of her eye.

A rider, picking his way through the trees.

For one heart-stopping moment, she thought maybe it was the man who'd taken Maddie, now coming for her.

But it only took that part of a second for her to recognize Collin, hatless and tall in the saddle.

Something caught in her chest, a burning knot of emotion that was locked there, as she turned Duncan to go meet him.

He must've seen her too, because he urged his horse faster.

He reined in and dismounted as she closed the last bit of distance between them.

He met her at Duncan's saddle, his eyes dark with concern. "You're hurt."

She threw her leg over the saddle. Collin caught her waist in his hands, carefully lowering her to the ground.

She reached her arms around his shoulders before her boots hit the dirt.

He held her close, turning his face into her neck. Hot breath tickled the place where her neck and shoulder met, but she didn't move.

She didn't ever want to move out of his embrace.

Tears filled her eyes. She squeezed them closed.

"I didn't think you'd come," she choked out, her face still buried against his chest.

"I'll always be here when you need me." He sounded a little choked up too.

He was the one who eased back.

Her arms fell away from his shoulders, and both his hands came up to cup her jaw. He tilted her head to look at her wound then breathed in through his teeth.

"What happened?"

"Duncan threw me," she said.

Collin tipped her head back so that she didn't have a choice but to look into his eyes. "Any other injuries?"

"I twisted my ankle. It's okay. Just a little tender." She rested her hands at his sides, content to just be.

Everything was still there. Maddie. That jewel. Irene.

But for this perfect second, she could rest in Collin's protective embrace.

He pressed a gentle kiss to her eyebrow, pressed his jaw to her forehead, away from her wound. "Duncan, huh?"

One of her tears slipped free. "I think we might've finally made our peace."

Saying the words was a reminder that she and Collin still had things unresolved between them.

She tipped her head up, looking into his dear face. Her feelings swirled inside her, ready to burst out.

"Collin, there are things I need to say to you. I—"

He silenced her with a kiss.

COLLIN WANTED nothing more than to hold on to Stella forever.

Seeing her with blood dried in the hair at her temple, her clothes dirty and rumpled... he'd felt a visceral need to protect her.

He tried to temper it in his kiss, didn't want to frighten her with the depths of his feelings.

He broke the kiss to brush smaller kisses along her jaw. He didn't want to let her go. "I was worried about you," he admitted against her ear.

"I—"

She broke off with a quick inhale of air as he ran his nose against her jaw. It made him smile.

But he also knew now wasn't the time.

There were shadows in her eyes when he pulled back.

"Collin, I made a mistake when I asked you to marry me."

Her words hit him in the soft solar plexus, and he went still. He didn't know what to say. It hurt.

He wanted to revisit that conversation. Wanted to change how he'd reacted.

She'd kissed him just now. It meant something. He knew it did.

"We can talk when we get back to camp," he said. "Where's Maddie?"

She shook her head. "I don't know. I thought I was following some tracks from camp, but—"

He squeezed her hand. "I smelled smoke. That was just before I saw you. I'd headed down into the gully to find it. We're too far from the wagon train for it to be from there. It's gotta be someone else."

She nodded, blinking away tears and firming her jaw.

"I'm here now," he said. "I'm not going anywhere. We'll get her back together."

She blew out a shuddery breath. "I'm ready."

He gave her a boost into the saddle, patting the stallion's shoulder before he stepped into his own saddle.

He turned his face into the slight breeze—it was stronger outside of the shelter of this gully—and scented a hint of sulphur again.

"Let's go," he said.

He and the gelding led the way. He checked over his shoulder every so often and found her riding with more confidence than before. The stallion, too, seemed calmer. Maybe they had made their peace.

The smell of smoke grew stronger as they approached a small ridge where the gully fell away.

Collin thought he heard a voice. He motioned for Stella to stop and reined in his gelding to dismount. He couldn't risk being seen, and the horses made them a bigger target.

They left the horses and did their best to stay hidden behind trees as they approached the ridge.

When his head cleared the lip of earth, he saw motion below and hunkered low. Stella followed suit.

They crawled forward a bit.

There was Maddie. Her hands and feet were bound

and she sat awkwardly on the ground a few feet away from a smoldering fire—one made with twigs and branches that were too wet and hadn't caught fire properly. It was all smoke and no flame. Couldn't do much with a fire like that.

A man with several days' worth of scruff on his chin stood over Maddie. Behind him, three saddled horses stood together, noses down toward the ground.

"Tell me where it is," the man threatened Maddie.

"I don't know!" Maddie's voice sounded teary.

The man leaned down and backhanded Stella's sister.

Stella made a sound like a stifled cry deep in her throat. She shuffled forward but Collin stayed her with a hand to her arm.

The last thing he needed was her showing their hiding spot or running down there and getting herself shot. The man had two six-shooters at his waist.

And someone who'd hit a helpless woman like that would have no compunction pulling a gun on one.

Collin kept hold of Stella's arm and carefully crawled back the way they'd come, at least far enough that they'd be out of sight and a whispered conversation wouldn't be overheard.

"There's only one man," she hissed.

He shook his head. "Three horses," he whispered.

She turned her head, like she could see over the edge again, when he knew she couldn't. "Where were they, then?" she demanded in a whisper.

"I don't know. Scouting? Looking for you?"

Tears stood in her eyes, but she bravely blinked them away. "We have to get her out of there. He hit her!"

"I saw," he said grimly. "I think you should ride back to camp and bring help."

She looked more uncertain about that than she had

about charging down the hill to face off with an evil man. "What if they don't believe me?"

He reached under the collar of his shirt and fished out the string that held his mother's ring. He tugged it over his head and then gently slipped it over hers.

She shook her head. "Collin, I can't—"

"Sure you can. Show it to Leo. To Coop, if he'll listen. Ask Leo to bring Owen and August and anybody else that'll come."

She glanced backward again. Worried about Maddie.

"I'll see what I can do to distract him. Try to get her out of there."

She squeezed her eyes shut. He knew he was asking a lot—for her to trust that he'd take care of her sister just like she would.

When she opened her eyes, they were filled with resolve. She surprised him by leaning forward and pressing a kiss against his lips.

"Don't die," she whispered fiercely.

He nodded gravely. "I won't."

He'd try his best, anyway.

He only watched her long enough to assure himself that she'd mounted up and started toward the wagon train before he crept back up the hill.

He wanted another look before he put himself in harm's way.

The man was railing at Maddie now as she cowered on the ground. "A month in this godforsaken wilderness." He spat on her. Collin's lip curled in disgust. "My boss wants his prize back, and I aim to bring it to him."

Maddie just shook her head. Was that a scrape on her cheek?

Collin felt protective anger surge through him.

At this moment, he could understand why Stella had done what she'd done. Why she'd hidden her true identity, why she'd asked him to marry her—when apparently that'd been a mistake, according to her.

She'd been trying to prevent *this*. Her deep love for her sisters was evident in everything she did. It made her reckless.

But he couldn't fault her for it.

And it only made him fall a little deeper in love with her.

How was he going to get Maddie away from that bad guy without getting himself shot?

NINETEEN

S tella disliked not having a plan. Or time to make a
plan.

But with Duncan racing at a gallop beneath
her, the two of them finally feeling like partners as she
leaned close over his neck, it seemed only minutes before
the circled wagons came into sight.

Only moments more and she was reining in near her
family's wagon. She saw Coop lounging with his back
against the Spencers' wagon, idly watching the cattle mill
about outside camp.

Where was Leo? Or Owen?

She stayed on horseback to make herself taller and
surveyed what she could see inside the circle.

There were more men around than usual.

Wait. These were uniformed men.

Soldiers from the fort? Why were they here?

She didn't see Leo anywhere. There was nothing for it.
She'd have to ask Coop.

She dismounted from Duncan, speaking softly to him,

telling him what a good boy he was as she tied him to the wagon.

"Stella?" Lily's head appeared from inside the wagon.

"Maddie's in trouble," Stella said. "Stay here with Irene."

"Wait—!"

But she couldn't. Her sister's cry trailed behind her. She heard rustling, like Lily was climbing out of the wagon, but she didn't have time to turn around and argue with her.

She strode over to Coop. "I need Leo."

He kept chewing his food, staring at her almost lazily.

His lack of response infuriated her. She wanted to knock some sense into him, but she needed his help. She barely kept a rein on her impatience.

"Maddie is in trouble," she said. "Collin sent me for help. They're both in danger."

She had his attention, but she didn't show him the ring Collin had pressed on her. She couldn't quite say why.

She could hear Lily coming up behind her.

"There's at least one man with a gun. He had Maddie tied up." She heard Lily gasp softly. She wasn't above begging. "Please, can you tell me where Leo is?"

An expression she couldn't read passed over his expression. So like Collin's, and yet so different.

He put his plate on the floor of the wagon bed behind him. "You left my brother out there alone?"

"With my sister," she reminded him. "Collin asked me to ride for help."

He put his hands on his hips, head down like he was thinking.

He wasn't thinking fast enough. All she needed to know was where Leo was. Or Owen.

She glanced over her shoulder to see Lily pale and

worried. If Coop wasn't going to help her, she'd find someone who would.

"Any idea where Leo or Owen is?"

Lily was already shaking her head.

Stella turned away from Coop, intent on her mission to find help.

But he grabbed her upper arm. He didn't hold on when she yanked away from him, and there'd been nothing unkind in his touch.

He stood closer than before. "Hang on a second—"

"No thank you," she said emphatically. "I love your brother. And if you're not going to point me to someone who can help him—"

He had a funny look on his face. Thoughtful, almost.

She was pointedly ignoring what she'd said. *I love your brother.*

And Lily's soft inhale that had followed on the heels of her admission. She hadn't meant to say that.

But it was true, wasn't it? Her stomach was twisted in knots as she worried about Collin and Maddie both.

"I never said I wasn't going to help you," he muttered. "Leo went off on a walk with Evangeline. All these soldiers filed into camp..."

Coop started walking into the center of the ring of wagons.

Lily held onto Stella's arm, pulling her back. "Stella—!"

"I know," she murmured. "We'll talk later."

The two of them followed a few steps behind Coop. He moved to interrupt a soldier who was talking with Elroy Jenkins.

"...looking for these criminals. Three of them. Do you recognize—?" The soldier was holding out a piece of paper.

A wanted poster, she realized with a slice of fear going through her.

She quickly turned away, ducking her head. She pulled Lily with her.

Three of them.

Was there a chance those wanted posters had a picture of Stella, Maddie, and Lily drawn on them? Irene had helped them, but they had committed a crime. They'd stolen money that wasn't theirs.

It'd felt like divine retribution at the time, a desperate decision she'd made to save her sisters.

But if the law was after them, all the way out here—?

"Stella—"

She shushed Lily, trying to think. But there was no solution easily forthcoming in her whirling thoughts.

Maddie.

Collin.

She had to think of her sister and of the man she loved. Even if it meant she went to jail. That was better than either of them dying, wasn't it?

She turned around again. Lily was looking at her askance. She must seem like a ninny.

Coop was talking to the soldier now, voices low enough that Stella couldn't hear.

But the soldier's hand had fallen to his side, giving her a glimpse of the hand-drawn portrait on that wanted poster.

"That's the man who has Maddie," she said.

Coop and the soldier looked up, broke off mid-sentence.

"That's him." She stepped closer, motioning frantically toward the poster. "He's got my sister. Collin was going to try to confront him."

The soldier raised up the poster and spread *three*

posters in his hands, holding them up for her to see as she neared. "Which one, miss?"

She pointed to the likeness of the man she'd seen. It was him, she was sure of it.

Coop sidled closer to her.

"Cyrus Bowder," she read off the poster.

"Why'd he grab your sister?" Coop asked. "Was one of the other men injured? Need medical help?" His question made sense, even if she hadn't thought about that angle until now.

Stella remembered Bowder's snarl, how he'd been pelting Maddie with questions about the ruby necklace.

"I—I don't know," she stammered. "I only saw him. No one else. Who is he?"

As if she didn't know. He was one of the Byrne brothers' men, sent after the four women.

The soldier whistled and several of his uniformed friends trotted over. "Him and his cronies are wanted in several states. Assault, murder. We got... erm, some information they were out here and might be aiming to rob one of the wagon trains."

That was confusing. Who would've tipped the soldiers off? Who else could've known what they'd be after? That they would be out here?

"Can you take us to them?" the soldier asked.

"Hang on," Coop said. His stance suddenly seemed more protective than anything else. "She isn't going to ride into danger."

The soldier sized him up.

"I only saw that man," she pointed to the poster again. "But there were three horses, and Collin thought maybe someone else was nearby."

Coop put a reassuring hand on her shoulder. "You

don't have to go back out there. Just tell us which direction to ride. We'll find them."

She didn't know what to do with this side of him. He seemed worried about her. Protective.

She tipped her chin up. Of course she wasn't going to stay here when Collin and Maddie were in danger. "I'll lead you back there."

Three murderers. Three men with guns.

And Maddie and Collin in their clutches.

She ran for the stallion.

COLLIN WATCHED from the top of that hill for longer than he wanted to.

Three horses, three saddles. Surely that meant three men. So where were the others?

The outlaw kept threatening Maddie. He hit her again, and it took everything in him not to rush down that hill.

The man had a gun. If he was any kind of shot at all and Collin put himself on the other end of a bullet, he wouldn't do Maddie any good.

How could he get down there without getting himself shot?

An idea came to him and since it was the only one he could think of and since no one else had appeared in the half hour since Stella had ridden off, he figured he had a chance.

He left his horse tied at a good distance, left his gun belt in the saddlebag. He quietly circled the camp, aiming to approach from the side. He used his pocketknife to cut a shallow gash under his hairline, knowing a head wound would bleed profusely.

It's what had scared him so badly when he'd gotten close enough to glimpse Stella.

He welcomed the blood running down his cheek. Picked up some mud and dirt and smeared it all on his clothes, made himself look more rumpled.

He stuffed his gun into the back waistband of his pants and hoped the outlaw wouldn't notice it. Hoping he wouldn't need to pull it at all.

When he got close enough to be noticed, he started limping, dragging his right foot behind him.

He heard the man's raised voice, saw him closing in on Maddie.

Collin groaned.

The man whirled, drawing his gun.

Collin didn't flinch. He pretended he hadn't noticed, held his left arm with his right hand as if he'd sprained that, too.

"S—Spencer, that you?" he called out.

"Don't come any closer," the man spat. His six-shooter was pointed straight at Collin.

He prayed harder than he ever had in his life. *Don't let him pull the trigger.*

"What—what day is it, friend?" Collin asked. He dragged his pretend limp a few feet closer. Still too far away.

Maddie was crumpled on the ground near that smoldering not-a-fire as she watched, terror-stricken. Even from here, he could see that the rope tying her legs had come loose. Could she get free?

"How many days since the twister?" Collin mumbled. "It picked me right up and tossed me like I was a straw doll. I been looking for the wagon train ever since."

"I ain't the wagon train," the outlaw said. "Now git."

Collin stopped, mostly because that six-shooter hadn't wavered a bit. He leaned against the nearest tree, squinting like he had the world's worst headache.

"Please—I need help. My wife..." He let himself wail a little.

If the outlaw had been spying on the wagon train enough to snatch Maddie in particular, he might recognize Collin. Especially since he and Coop stood out, as twins.

Collin couldn't afford to be recognized.

"I said git." The man fired a warning shot that kicked up dirt only a few feet in front of Collin.

Maddie cried out. One of her feet slipped out of the rope.

Collin's heart was racing, and it was everything he could do to not react. He clumsily half-sat, half-fell on the ground. "I can barely walk, and my arm..." He winced internally. Better not to draw attention to his arm. It wasn't really hurt. "I ain't ate in three days." Was he playing this too over-the-top? Would his voice be weaker if he hadn't eaten in such a long time?

"If I did have any food, I wouldn't be sharing it," the outlaw growled.

Maddie had shuffled a few inches. The outlaw turned to glare at her. "You wanna get shot? Be still."

He didn't have any food. Maybe Collin could use that.

"I h-hate it out here," Collin whimpered. He imagined he was Braddock, the stupid city-slicker. "My wife's the one who wanted to come west and now look what's happened. D'you know—what happened to her?"

Collin didn't have to pretend to put the emotion in his voice. He was scared to death for Maddie. And Stella. Stella would never recover if he couldn't get Maddie away from the outlaw.

"I don't know you or your wife," the outlaw said, voice rising. "And I ain't asked to be out here, neither. Sleepin' in the dirt. No food. Drinkin' from the creek like a *dog*."

He lowered his gun, but Collin didn't have time to be relieved because he stalked toward Maddie, who was still shuffling a slow inch-by-inch.

The outlaw kicked her in the thigh. She cried out.

"This is all your fault! Where's the ruby?"

He pointed his gun at her now.

Collin was afraid of the desperation in the outlaw's voice. He'd meant to distract the man, meant to keep his attention off Maddie, but that's not what had happened.

Collin pushed himself up, using the tree as leverage.

The outlaw was still focused on Maddie.

Collin shuffled forward, dragging his leg but moving more quickly than he had before.

"What're you—?" Now the outlaw swung so his gun was pointed at Collin again.

"Please. You got a fire." Collin dragged himself forward another step. "I know you got some kind of food." Another, bracing for a shot all the while. "Hardtack or a biscuit. Just one bite—"

"Git back!" The outlaw roared.

"Hey!" A male voice called out, and for one glorious moment, Collin thought he was saved.

But when he turned his head, he saw a man he didn't recognize, a man with a full, dark beard and a rumpled three-piece suit, running up on foot. He had his six-shooter pointed at Collin.

Another outlaw.

Collin's hope withered. He'd thought Stella had sent one of his brothers. Not that he wanted either of them in danger, or anyone else from the wagon train.

Should he keep playacting?

The second outlaw, Mr. Beard, moved to stand near the first man.

"He says he's lookin' for food," the first outlaw said.

"The twister—" Collin started, but Mr. Beard shook his head.

"I've seen you around camp," he said.

Oh no.

Collin was still too far away.

But with the two outlaws distracted, Maddie had gotten into a crouch, her skirt in hands, like she was ready to run.

There was a hollow not far behind her. It wouldn't provide much protection.

But maybe he could take one of the men out with him.

"Shoot him—"

Mr. Beard hadn't got the words out before Collin reached behind his waist.

"Maddie, run!" He twisted and lurched, drawing his weapon as a shot rang out.

Fire streaked up his left arm as he got off two shots, being careful to keep his aim away from Maddie darting away behind the two outlaws.

He couldn't risk one of them shooting at her, so Collin charged forward and to the side, making himself a bigger target.

He had a clear view of the first outlaw. He squeezed the trigger.

Just as another shot rang out.

TWENTY

"Collin!"

He was in motion as he heard Stella's cry from some distance.

Worry and fury kept him moving. Was she alone? Was she in danger?

"Stop shooting! Lay down your weapons!"

Collin ducked behind a skinny poplar as a man's voice rang out.

"You're surrounded!"

The bullets stopped flying, and Collin dared to glance around the edge of the tree.

He saw six or seven men in cavalry uniforms on horseback. Several of them aiming rifles at the two outlaws.

Who scowled but put their six-shooters on the ground.

Collin bent to set his revolver down, just to be safe.

Then there was Stella, flying down the hill on her stallion. Was that...? Coop, keeping pace on his horse beside her. Collin was shocked to see his twin.

His arm ached, but he turned his attention to the spectacle in front of him.

"Maddie?" he called out.

Stella was already off her horse and rushing to his side, reaching for him. "You're hurt."

He shifted her behind him so any rogue bullets that came flying would hit him first.

Coop arrived close behind her.

Collin shot his twin a scathing look. "You let her ride down here into danger?"

Coop pulled a face. "You think you could've stopped her?"

Stella had a grip on his wrist. "Stop speaking as if I'm not here. Let me see this." She'd unbuttoned his cuff and was attempting to roll up his sleeve.

"Go check on Maddie," he told her. "I'm all right."

But when her eyes flashed up to him, he saw the worry in their depths.

His arm throbbed as he squeezed her elbow with his other hand. "I'm all right. Coop can look after me for a minute. Your sister needs you."

That seemed to galvanize her, and she left him with one last lingering look.

Coop raised one speaking eyebrow. "You want me to doctor you?"

Collin looked down to where he was bleeding through his shirt. "Bullet grazed me, I think. What's the cavalry doing here?"

Coop lowered his voice. "They came into camp earlier. Had three wanted posters. Stella swears one of those men shooting at you was on the posters."

Collin shook his head. What in the world? How did

soldiers from the fort get wanted posters for the New Yorkers who were after Stella and her sisters?

"Anything you wanna tell me?" Coop asked. He was squinting a little, watching as the soldiers closed in on the two gunslingers.

"No."

Stella came back to them, her arm around Maddie, whose face was already showing signs of purple bruises on her jaw. Collin wanted to pummel the man who'd done that to her.

"Are you all right?" Stella asked him, quickly going on. "Of course you aren't." She looked like she wanted to cry.

"I'm alive. That's enough. Lily all right?"

Stella nodded, and a tear slipped down her cheek.

One of the men, this one a little older than the others judging by the bushy gray mustache, rode up to them while one of the outlaws struggled with two soldiers as they held his hands to tie them.

Another soldier kicked dirt on the smoldering fire.

"You mixed up in this?" The older soldier asked them.

"Only trying to help," Collin said. Stella and Maddie moved to stand next to him.

"Pretty daring to confront two notorious criminals with guns."

"Didn't have much choice," Collin said. "He pulled his gun on an innocent woman."

"They ain't innocent," Mr. Beard called out. "They stole a ten thousand dollar ruby necklace from my—from a friend of mine. He sent me to get it back."

Stella and Maddie exchanged a split-second glance.

The older soldier's gaze landed on Stella. "That true?"

Coop let out a guffaw. Stella jumped.

Collin let his hand slide down to wrap his fingers around hers. Her skin was cold to the touch.

"If she stole some jewel, she'd have sold it to pay for this trip."

The outlaw tried to shrug off the solder who was leading him toward the horses. It didn't work. "That jewel is worth far more than a wagon and supplies."

Collin saw the twitch of Coop's hand—his tell. What did he know about the necklace?

"You got his fancy necklace?" Coop asked Stella.

She shook her head. Her face was pale, her eyes wide in her face.

"What about you?" Coop pointed this question at Maddie, who also shook her head.

"I don't know anything about a necklace," the soldier said. "But I know you boys are wanted for murder. You're coming back to the fort with us."

The pain in Collin's arm was beginning to pulse on each heartbeat, really starting to sting now. He shifted his feet.

Coop glanced at him. Frowned.

"Search their wagon," Mr. Beard said. He sure was bossy for someone who had a couple of rifles aimed in his direction. "I know she has the necklace. I want it back."

"Weren't there three wanted posters?" Coop asked. "Where's that other man?"

The soldier frowned. "You ain't in charge, sonny." But he looked thoughtful. "We'll get these two back to camp I'll send out a few men to search."

He turned his focus to Stella, "Mind showing us your wagon?"

Maddie started to say something, but Stella squeezed her hand. "All right."

Maddie whispered something in Stella's ear, but she shook her head. "Collin was shot. His wound needs caring for."

STELLA MOUNTED UP AND WAITED.

It was only a few seconds before Collin stepped into the saddle behind her.

Duncan didn't balk at having two riders in the saddle, and that was a relief. But not as much relief as having Collin, big and warm and real, sitting behind her.

His right hand settled at her waist. It reminded her that his other arm was injured.

"Is your arm—?"

He squeezed her waist gently. "It'll keep."

Coop helped Maddie onto Collin's horse that had been retrieved from the woods. He rode next to her, conscientious.

Stella nudged Duncan into a walk, following the soldiers. They'd tied the two gunslingers' hands in front of them and put them on horses that two of the soldiers led.

Stella couldn't help examining Maddie's face again, anxiously searching every puffy bruise forming. Was her sister really all right? There hadn't been time to talk about the ordeal she'd survived.

She couldn't seem to stop shaking, even with Collin's body warming her back.

He gently coaxed her to lean against him, moving so that his arm was around her waist, his hand splayed over her belly.

"It's going to be all right," he whispered into her ear, his cheek pressed against the side of her head. "I'm not going to let anything happen to you."

"It's not that. I can't stop thinking about you getting shot." She shuddered as the memory played behind her eyes again.

The gunslingers' six-shooter kicked, a muzzle-flash of fire, a terrible noise of gunfire. Collin had been diving out of the way, but she'd seen his body jerk.

She'd thought he'd been killed, especially when everything had gone quiet and still.

"I'm here." His whispered words were a warm breath against her ear. "Nothing bad happened to me."

"You got shot," she countered. "That's plenty bad." Coop had tied a makeshift bandage around Collin's arm when they'd come back to the horses. Even with the bandage, she was worried that he was still bleeding, or that infection would set in.

Collin's head inched forward even as his hand left her middle. He reached up to tip her chin and because they were sitting so close and he was so tall, it seemed easy enough to tilt her head and meet his kiss.

She felt the catch in his breath as she kissed him back, and that, plus the way his fingers slid under her braid to sift into her hair, was such a vivid reminder that he was alive that she could soar with joy.

A pointed throat clearing nearby broke through the idyllic moment. Collin pulled away.

He stared down at her, affection and warmth on his expressive face. It was easier to look at him than meet what must be the curious stare of Coop—who'd made that sound.

But she couldn't crane her neck like this forever, so she settled with her back against Collin's chest once again.

Collin was already whispering against her ear again. "I think we should get married."

What? Her heart thumped even louder than when he'd kissed her.

"But you said—"

He hugged her with his good arm. "I know what I said. I was wrong. You were right."

She didn't have time to savor the moment of him saying that because he was still speaking.

"My family has good standing. You and your sisters will have my protection. It makes sense, just like you said."

He sounded sincere. His voice was calm and decisive.

And with each word he spoke, her heart sank.

She'd known her proposal to him had been logical and even... mercenary.

But hearing it from his lips... there had been nothing about his feelings. His heart.

She should be grateful. Relieved.

But it was a bitter disappointment that she swallowed.

I love your brother, she'd told Coop.

Coop.

Would he tell Collin what she'd said? She knew that the brothers used to be close.

She should just tell Collin. Right now.

I love you.

But the words wouldn't emerge.

She'd been so full of joy and relief when she'd seen Collin stand up from behind that tree. Everything she'd felt for him had become crystal clear, and she'd thrown herself at him.

But he'd quickly urged her to check on Maddie.

What if... what if she was wrong? What if he didn't feel the same way about her?

Thinking that was almost as terrifying as seeing him shot.

Could she marry him, knowing she felt far more for him than he did for her?

He spoke again. "We'll get back and let Irene explain herself. Then we can talk to Hollis. I don't want to wait for the next Sunday worship. He can marry us tonight."

He can marry us tonight.

Stella's heart was pounding now for the wrong reasons. "Collin, I—"

She didn't know what she'd meant to say. That she couldn't go through with it. She'd never technically agreed with his plans, made just now on horseback.

But the circled wagons were in sight. And the soldiers had surrounded them, Coop and Maddie were *right there.*

She couldn't find the words to fix this.

And maybe a part of her, a very selfish little part, wanted to go through with it. Marry Collin. Maybe... eventually... he'd fall in love with her too.

Lily had been standing near Alice and Leo at their campfire. When she caught sight of the procession riding in to camp, she rushed forward.

Leo and Alice followed.

"Stella! Maddie!" Lily's voice was wet with tears and relief.

"What happened?" Leo demanded as he caught sight of Collin's bloodied sleeve.

"Collin!" Alice cried out.

They dismounted in chaos. Lily pulled Maddie into her embrace. Maddie began recounting everything that had happened since she'd been snatched.

All of it made Stella a little dizzy. And when the sergeant looked at her, she swallowed hard.

"Our wagon is that one." She pointed, then started walking.

What was she going to do when he found Irene and the necklace inside? She and her sisters would look guilty. Maybe they were guilty, since they'd unknowingly been a part of the theft.

Collin walked close beside her, his hand at her waist.

She should tell him to keep his distance right now. She didn't want him implicated in whatever was about to happen.

"There's a woman inside," she told the soldier. "Irene. She's been very ill."

He knocked once on the side of the wagon. "Ma'am?"

There was no answer.

He loosened the canvas covering so he could see inside. It truly did smell like sickness, and she saw the slight curl of his lip in distaste.

He swept back the covering.

And the wagon was empty.

The soldier looked at her. She was totally confused.

"Lily?"

A glance at her sister, who'd trailed behind and still had her arms around Maddie's waist, showed that Lily was as shocked as she was.

"She was in there, lying down, last time I checked on her," Lily said.

Last time Stella had seen Irene, the woman could barely walk, had been doubled over with stomach pain. Where could she have gone?

Could she have just walked off without anyone knowing?

It seemed preposterous.

"You mind if we search the wagon?" the soldier asked.

He didn't give Stella a chance to answer before he began rifling through their belongings.

It made her sort of sick to watch so she turned her face away.

That wasn't any better. Collin was right there, and she couldn't tell if his shirt was more blood-soaked than before.

"Maddie, can you doctor him?"

Her sister nodded, a determined set to her lips.

"It can wait," Collin said.

"No, it can't." There were tears in her eyes as she pushed him toward Maddie. "We need to make sure you don't get an infection."

He brushed a kiss on her forehead. "I won't be far."

The sergeant stepped back from her wagon, shaking his head.

The man who'd been on one of those posters and the one who'd shot Collin, called out, "I know she has it!"

"There's nothing here," said the sergeant. "It's time to get those two outlaws to the fort."

TWENTY-ONE

Collin winced as the medic from Fort Kearny stitched him up. He was laid out on an infirmary bed that felt more like a wooden plank and his wound stung from the strong disinfectant the man had poured on it after he'd fished out the bullet.

Fort Kearny was a series of buildings in a neat square surrounding a parade ground. Most of them must be barracks, he thought, though there were several officers' quarters and a post office.

Collin hadn't really registered all of it due to the pain pulsing all throughout his arm.

Turned out the bullet hadn't just grazed him. It'd lodged in the fleshy part of his arm. Maddie had taken one look at it back at camp and told him she didn't have the right tools for surgery like he needed.

That was about the same time as the hired gun he'd taken to calling Mr. Beard had put up a fuss.

Irene was missing, and the sergeant had searched the women's wagon and found nothing.

Which made the gunslinger he now knew as Gabriel Griffin furious. "They stole it. It's here somewhere."

You got this fancy-schmancy necklace he's talking about?

It'd been Coop's calm and collected question, directed at Stella, that'd broken the tension that seemed at its boiling point.

No.

Stella's answer had been clear and calm, too.

It didn't take long before the handful of soldiers the sergeant had dispatched returned. Empty-handed. Irene had disappeared. And the plains were too big to keep searching for one woman.

Collin'd been so intent on listening and watching what was happening with Stella that he hadn't realized Leo and Owen had come over to talk to Maddie, who informed them she couldn't fix Collin up.

The two half-brothers had a quick conversation and left to tell the travelers to pack up. They were all moving to the fort, under Hollis's direction. Hollis would make any further decisions from here.

Collin's skin pulled as the medic's stitching wasn't exactly gentle. The man didn't seem that old, but he was grizzled and his skin looked like leather. And he was missing a front tooth. Maybe that's why Collin wasn't enjoying his ministrations as much as he would've if Maddie'd been doctoring him up.

And he was plenty irritated that he didn't know where Stella was and decisions were being made without him.

"Be still," the doc growled.

Collin hadn't realized he'd moved before, but now he craned his neck to try and see out the open door. Leo'd brought him into the fort. Where was his brother? Maybe Leo knew where Stella was.

A shadow moved, and there was Leo, striding into the room. He looked grim. Almost as grim as he had that night in New Jersey. It'd been Coop causing trouble then.

But now Leo's concern was aimed right at Collin, whose stomach twisted.

"How's it look?" Leo asked.

"I'm fine," Collin said. "He's almost done."

"Be done faster if you'd *stop moving*," the doctor growled again.

The room went silent until Leo said, "I'd like to hear from the medic."

"Bullet came out. Disinfected it—"

"With a bucket of medicine," Collin complained.

"—and now stitching him up. As long as he don't get an infection, he should be fine."

Leo's brows creased. No doubt he was thinking the same thing Collin was. That the trail was dusty and dirty.

"I'll be careful," Collin said. "Keep it bandaged real nice and clean."

Stella had been worried about infection too.

"Where's Stella? She all right?"

The doc sighed. Collin must've moved again, but at least the man was finally tying off his thread.

Leo crossed his arms over his chest. "Sergeant spoke to her. And her sisters. Something's going on with them, but they're not talking much. You wanna tell me anything?"

"No. I wanna see her." Collin pushed up to a seated position as the medic stepped away.

"I know you fancy her, but maybe it'd be best—"

"It'd be best if you stay out of it," he told Leo quietly.

He was deadly serious. "I don't just fancy her. I'm in love with her."

Leo had that look on his face, the same one he wore when Coop did something stupid. Like he'd swallowed something sour mixed with dirt and chased it down with leftover dishwater. "Collin—"

"You don't know her," he argued. "She's a lot like you, actually. Maybe even tougher than you. She's had to scrap and work harder than any man just to survive." She hadn't told him everything. He was sure of that. But someone desperate enough to steal food so they wouldn't starve must've been willing to do just about anything to keep them safe and alive.

"Give her half a chance. You'll like her," Collin said. "She's whip-smart and kind and a little shy."

Leo dropped his hands then rubbed one down his face. His shoulders drooped like he was suddenly exhausted. "Please tell me I didn't sound this besotted when I was courting Evangeline."

"When did you court her?" Collin teased. "Between all the pretending?"

Leo made a gurgling growl. "Are you sure you know what you're doing?"

"My brain? No. But my heart is sure."

And that was enough.

Leo sighed. "The soldiers are keeping Bowder and Griffin in the guardhouse prison cell until the commanding officer decides what to do with them."

That sounded promising. But—

"What about that other wanted poster? Wasn't there a third man chasing the women?"

Leo shrugged. "Neither the soldiers nor anyone from the wagon train has seen another man."

"Do you think he grabbed Irene?"

Leo shook his head. "I don't know. Maybe she ran. Did she have a reason to run?"

Collin shrugged. "How should I know?" There he went, avoiding the question, just like Coop. Maybe things weren't always black and white.

Collin attempted to stand up but the moment his boots hit the floor, he got woozy. He wobbled. Thankfully, Leo was there with a hand under his elbow, steadying him.

"Easy," Leo said. "You've lost some blood. You need to rest."

But Collin couldn't afford to rest. Stella needed him. And he'd had a thought just before the dizziness hit. What was it—?

"Who brought those wanted posters all the way out here?" he wondered aloud.

"Captain said it was a private investigator."

"Who paid for that? Why was he out here?" Collin had to put a hand to his aching head.

"There's plenty of time to figure that out later. You need to be in your bedroll."

"I need to see Stella."

Leo nodded to the doorway. "Here she is. Now let me help you walk so we can get outta here."

There she was indeed. She had worry lines around her mouth, her eyes were luminous with tears.

He was still wobbly as Leo helped him toward the door. Stella quickly moved to slide against his other side, her arm wrapping around his waist.

"What happened with the soldiers?" he asked.

"Later," she promised. "Your brother is right. You need to rest."

STELLA WOKE with a sense that something was very wrong.

She hadn't meant to sleep. She was still propped against the wagon wheel of her own wagon, her chin resting on her sternum. She'd sat here to watch over Collin, resting in his bedroll nearby.

She and Leo had helped Collin to the campsite, but by the time they'd reached the wagons, Collin had been out of it, mumbling nonsense. He'd settled in his bedroll easy enough when she'd assured him they would talk in the morning.

Had he made some noise of discomfort? Was that what had woken her?

Motion from close beside her sent prickles of unease racing across her skin.

Before she could so much as move, something cold and thin pressed against her neck.

"Don't move. Don't even twitch."

Recognition flared.

"Irene?" she whispered.

The blade at her throat ticked, like the woman's hand had spasmed.

How had Irene snuck so close? Stella must have been deeper asleep than she'd thought.

"Where's my ruby?" Irene demanded.

"I thought you had it."

It was the wrong answer. Irene's hand tangled in Stella's hair. She resisted the urge to cry out as Irene yanked her head back. The knife bit into her skin though she didn't think she'd been cut yet.

Her mind raced. Collin was asleep nearby—and he was

injured. Maddie and Lily were huddled together closer to the dying fire.

No one knew Stella was being held at knife point. What could she do?

"I snuck outta the wagon when I heard the soldiers in camp. Couldn't risk them finding me. Sick as a dog and you took it off my neck."

Irene seemed to be mumbling that last part to herself.

"I didn't take it," Stella said. "Maybe it fell off."

Irene's hand shook. "Well, where is it, then? Somewhere in the wagon?"

Stella dared to shake her head slightly. "The soldiers searched through the wagon earlier. Two of the Byrne brothers' men kidnapped Maddie. They shot Collin."

If she'd hoped to play on Irene's sympathy, it didn't work.

"They'll do worse than that if they find me." Irene's voice shook. Her hand did too. This time Stella felt the bite of a shallow cut. "I want my ruby, then I'll disappear for good."

How was Irene going to do that? She seemed muddled. Maybe it was the fever or sickness that made her so.

"I need it, I need it," she whispered desperately. Then, louder, "if you ain't got it, maybe one of your sisters does. Maybe I'll use this knife on them and—"

"No." Stella's voice was sharp in the darkness. She held her breath. She didn't know whether to hope she might wake someone or pray that no one stirred.

Everything was silent.

"I'll help you. I remembered something." She needed to keep Irene away from her sisters, away from Collin.

She had one wild idea that might just work.

"Can we stand up? Can you take the knife away?"

Irene didn't move. Had she heard? Was she lost in thoughts?

"We helped each other in New York, didn't we?" It was difficult to make her voice sound friendly when Irene was acting like this, after what she'd done. "We worked together then, and we'll do the same now."

Irene let go of her hair. The blade moved away from her throat.

Stella had put away her gun earlier, when the Byrnes' men had been safely in custody. Even if she'd had it, she wouldn't have taken the risk of trying to shoot in the dark, with so many people around.

But she'd kept her knife in her pocket. She could feel its weight there now as she carefully stood up. She didn't dare reach for it.

Not yet.

"This way." She took two steps away from the wagon, toward where the horses were picketed.

"Wait a second—" Irene grabbed her arm.

At the same moment, Stella whistled. The same two-tone whistle Collin had taught her.

She didn't know whether it would work. She braced herself for the searing pain of a knife stabbing her—

Then Duncan appeared, a darker shadow against the night sky. He gave a fearsome neigh and ran right up to them.

Irene gasped. Her hand fell away.

Duncan butted his chest into Irene. She fell onto her hindquarters even as Stella reached for the rope around the horse's neck.

Duncan pranced in place, his hooves coming danger-ously close to Irene, who scrambled away, still on her backside.

"Easy, boy," Stella said.

The horse stood between Stella and the tiny amount of light from the camp's dying fires. Stella couldn't see Irene any longer.

"Irene?"

"She better be making tracks." The sound of a cocked revolver punctuated Collin's words. "And not come back," he called out softly into the night. "If I see you again, I won't hesitate to shoot."

"Collin." She didn't know whether he heard her. He walked a big circle around where she stood. She tried to stop shaking as she settled Duncan.

As Collin approached, he gently put the hammer back down on his revolver and slid the gun back in its holster.

"Come here," Collin said.

Duncan was fine now, and Stella was more than happy to be pulled into Collin's embrace.

"Are you all right?" he asked the question into her hair.

She shook her head.

He rubbed her arms, and she was content to let him lead her back to the fire. She greedily soaked up the sight of both her sisters sleeping undisturbed. She wouldn't be falling asleep again tonight.

Collin bypassed her fire to go to his own family's. Everything was quiet there, a soft snore coming from the nearest tent.

Collin stirred up the ashes, dislodging a couple of coals. He fed in some kindling and soon a small amount of warmth permeated the air.

She felt him look at her from where he squatted near the fire, but she could only stare at the flames as she tried to process what had just happened.

"Are you...?" He paused for a beat. "Are you wearing a dress?"

She blushed, brushing at her skirt idly. "Don't tease."

"I won't. I just..." He didn't say *what* he was *just*. "I've never seen you in a dress."

He probably couldn't see much in the dark. The fire wasn't bright yet. Clouds covered the sky, blocking the moon and stars.

She ducked her head, waiting for him to say something. Not sure whether she wanted him to compliment her or say that she looked silly. Like someone playing dress up.

He came to sit next to her, his hand closing over hers. His skin was warm to the touch. She felt like a block of ice inside.

"Trousers or dress, you always look beautiful to me," he said.

Her gaze darted to him. His hair and clothes were rumpled. A pink line down one cheek showed just how hard he'd been sleeping.

"It's true. You're the most beautiful thing I've ever seen."

His words fell like water on a parched garden. She soaked them up, treasuring them in her heart.

He squeezed her hand. "She came looking for her necklace, I take it?"

Her gaze traversed his face. "You knew?"

"Lily and I saw it. We tried to rouse her just before I came hunting for you."

She shook her head, unable to make sense of it. He hadn't breathed a word to the soldiers, not that she was aware of.

"I wanted to tell you," she whispered. "I only found out when she got so sick."

"That necklace was why the gunslingers were chasing you."

She nodded. A late wave of fear over what could've happened swept over her. She shivered.

He let go of her hand and tucked her under his arm, next to his side. He inhaled sharply.

"Collin. Your arm."

He held her when she would've wiggled away. "I'm fine."

That's not what Leo had said as they'd worked together to tuck Collin into his bedroll. The medic from the fort was worried about infection.

She pinched his thigh when he still wouldn't let her go, but gently. "You should go back to bed."

Maddie had told her that losing blood like he had from his wound might make him tired for a few days and that he'd need to drink a lot of water.

"In a minute."

"Are you in much pain?" When she tilted her head, she could see how pale he still was.

He gave her a mischievous sideways smirk. "If I say yes, will you kiss me until I'm better?"

She nudged his side with her elbow, and he gave a pretend pained gasp.

"You don't have to be injured to receive kisses," she told him, though it was easier to gaze into the fire than meet his eyes when she said it.

He looked at her, but when she kept staring at the fire, he looked there too. "No?"

"No." She shifted slightly closer and leaned her head so it was resting on his shoulder.

She felt the movement of his throat as if he swallowed hard. "So you'll marry me?"

"Yes," she whispered.

"Stella." He shifted, dislodging her from against him. He lifted his hand to cup her cheek and leaned in for a kiss.

She curled against his chest, one hand slipping to hold the back of his neck while the other rested on his shoulder.

This was what love felt like. But there was so much she needed to say.

She gently pushed him away. "I'm not marrying you because it's convenient," she said.

He looked a little dazed, and she felt warm that she could make him so.

"All those reasons I gave you why getting married makes sense... I don't care about them."

Now he looked bemused. "Me neither."

"Then why did you recount them when we were riding back?"

"You made everything sound so logical," he said. "I thought being logical would be the best way to convince you."

She stared at his dear face, revealed in the flickering firelight.

"So then, if you're not marrying me for logic," he said. "Why are you marrying me?"

Her face grew hot. But she wasn't scared anymore to say the words. "Because I love you."

Some fine tension left him. He grinned at her. "You do, huh? Because I'm so charming? So handsome?"

She resisted the urge to pinch him for real. But for only a second or two.

"Ow!"

"Ssh. You'll wake everyone up," she said.

He was still grinning when he brushed a kiss on her cheek. "I love you, too, you know."

He did?

She'd hoped, wanted it fiercely even though she hadn't admitted it to herself.

He brushed a strand of hair out of her eyes. "There was something about you that made me notice you, even before I knew the real Stella. And once you stopped hiding the real you, well... it didn't take long for me to fall in love with you."

His words were everything she hadn't known she needed to hear.

"I want to stand by your side. Take care of you."

She nodded through tears making her eyes hot. "I want to do the same for you."

"But right now, I want to kiss you again."

She didn't argue.

TWENTY-TWO

C ollin woke with the first rays of light streaking across the sky. He glanced to where Stella had finally settled into his bedroll a few feet away. He could barely believe what had happened in the night had been real.

Irene—

Then him finally saying the right words.

Stella was going to marry him.

He stretched on the ground, his injured arm throbbing when he accidentally rolled over on it. He stifled a groan in his closed fist.

There were folks moving around camp. Preparing for the day. Quietly making breakfast.

Because the travelers had arrived at the fort so late, Hollis had agreed to let everyone have a half day to purchase what they needed before the wagon train moved on.

Which meant Collin had half a day to secure Stella's future in the wagon train. Nothing had changed. Hollis hadn't made any decisions about what to do with her. Would she be left behind when the wagon train rolled out?

He sat up, rubbing his face.

When he'd fallen asleep after sitting with Stella at the fire, Coop's bedroll had been empty. He'd been on watch and keeping track of the cattle.

Now he was in his bedroll a few feet away from the family's tent, one arm bent behind his head. He seemed to be awake.

Collin crept to crouch over his saddlebags. Coop shifted to look at him in the dim morning light.

Collin hadn't yet had a chance to talk to his brother about the events of yesterday. "Why'd you help Stella?" he asked as he pulled a clean shirt from his supplies.

Today was definitely a day for a clean shirt.

"Because she matters to you." Coop said the words in a careful, calm voice.

Because I love you. He would never forget last night, the first time he'd heard the words from her. The tremble in her voice. The joy that had surged through him.

Nor could he forget the words his brother had hurled at him. *You care more about a pretty face than your brother.*

Had Coop helped Stella as a way of apologizing for his earlier behavior?

"You're gonna marry her," Coop said now, shifting so he was staring up at the brightening sky.

"Yes." Collin worked to unbutton his shirt. Every movement of his injured arm caused a flare of pain.

"I like her," Coop announced. "Even though you won't be my brother any more."

Sliding the old shirt off wasn't so bad, but when he moved wrong while pulling the new shirt over his arm, he had to bite back a cry as white hot pain flared. "What are you talking about? We'll always be brothers."

Coop rolled his head back and forth on his arm, the movement a little too exaggerated. "No, sirree."

Suspicion stirred, twisting Collin's stomach.

"We haven't been brothers since New Jersey," Coop said. His careful enunciation slipped. He began to slur. "And now she's taking you away from me for good."

With the hand not trapped behind his head, Coop lifted a silver flask to his lips and took a swig.

Collin strode over and kicked the flask out of his hand. It landed on the ground a few feet away. Clear liquid slowly *glugged* out.

"You're drunk." Collin made no effort to hide his disgust.

Coop sat up, his bedroll twisted around him. His cheeks were flushed and his eyes glassy.

"No 'm not. I jus'—jus' lifted a glass to celebrate your impending—"

"Don't make excuses." Collin stepped back, fingers fumbling to button his shirt. Where was Leo? Probably with the cattle. He hated to wake Alice to deal with Coop like this. It would break her heart to see him drunk.

"Why'd you kick my whiskey?" Coop's temper flared.

Collin felt his going up in flames to match. "Why do you keep doing this? Why do you want to tear our family apart?"

Coop rose to his knees, his legs still tangled in his bedroll. "I'm not the one tearing it apart. *You're* the one getting married. Leaving me."

I'm not leaving you. Collin didn't say the words because he couldn't guarantee they were true. Stella hadn't spoken to Hollis yet. There'd been no decision on whether she and her sisters could stay with the wagon train. And if she were turned away... well, he'd made his promise to her, even if they hadn't exchanged vows yet.

A gentle hand touched his back. Collin had been so focused on his brother and his anger that he hadn't noticed Stella's approach. She stood close beside him, leaning in to him to offer him support.

Her presence instantly calmed him. He breathed deeply. Remembered what was important.

"There she is," Coop said. "The blushing bride."

Collin looked down into Stella's dear face. As she gazed up at him, he saw her sorrow and hurt—for him.

"He needs to sleep it off," she murmured.

"See, she's already like a sister," Coop said. "Telling me what to do."

Collin stared at Stella for another moment, taking strength from her presence. And then he squatted so he was face to face with Coop.

"We were born brothers. And we'll die brothers," he said in as serious a voice he could muster. "I'm not ever going to stop loving you, no matter what you do."

Coop fell back on his rump, all the anger draining out of him. He glared at Collin, but there was no malice in it.

"I want you to clean up your act," Collin went on. "For yourself. Are you really happy, living like this?"

Coop's expression shifted to stubborn determination. "Course I am. Why wouldn't I be?" He lifted the corner of the bedroll to cover his face and laid back down. "I'm gonna catch a few hours before we have to pack up."

Guess that was the end of the conversation.

Collin shook his head as he straightened.

And Stella was still there, waiting for him. Understanding when he needed a moment to catch his breath from the unexpected hurt of the moment.

She was holding something behind her back.

"What do you have there?" he asked.

"A gift for you." She extended it in front of her.

A new hat, a fancy felt one that looked like it'd never been worn before.

He took it from her, rotating it in his hands.

"Lily bought it for me in the fort, last night while you were in the medic's office."

"You didn't have to—"

"I wanted to." She lifted her chin with that endearing stubbornness.

And he found himself smiling at her. He held out his hand. "Are you ready?"

Her hand was trembling slightly when she put it in his. "Are you certain?"

"I am."

She released some tension with her exhale.

It only took a few minutes to walk to the fort. Another few to locate the chaplain, who was eating breakfast. He seemed indifferent to their request until Collin proffered two dollar bills.

They followed him outside, where he flagged down two passing soldiers.

The wedding ceremony was a far cry from Leo's only a week ago.

But Collin felt the gravity of the moment the same as he had when he'd stood up for his brother.

Will you take this woman to be your wife? To live together in holy matrimony?

It was easy to say yes.

Will you take this man to be your husband? To live together in holy matrimony?

There was something about Stella's soft *yes* that hit him hard. He found himself blinking back moisture.

When the chaplain asked them to repeat their vows, he had to clear his throat.

"I take you as my wedded wife... to have and to hold... from this day forward... for better, for worse... for richer and poorer... in sickness and health... to love and to cherish... till death do us part."

He squeezed Stella's hands in his when it was her turn. "I take you as my wedded husband... to have and to hold... from this day forward... for better, for worse... for richer and poorer... in sickness and health... to honor and obey... till death do us part."

And then they both glanced at the chaplain, who gave a simple nod. "That's it. You're hitched."

Collin didn't know what he'd expected, but too late he remembered the silver band he'd given Stella.

"Wait." He looked at her. "Do you still have my ring?"

She flushed prettily. "Yes, but—"

"Can I have it?"

"Collin." Her protest was soft as she took the leather strap from beneath her collar. She gave it to him. It was the work of a moment to untie it. He held it up for the chaplain to see.

The man nodded.

"Collin," Stella said in a hushed voice.

"This was my grandmother's. I want you to have it." He pushed the simple gold band onto her finger. Alice had given it to him on his fifteenth birthday. She'd passed their mother's ring to Coop at the same time.

Now Stella was the one blinking back tears. The chaplain had said they were hitched, so Collin tugged Stella in to collect a tender kiss.

Their witnesses didn't seem to care, and neither did the chaplain, so he gave her one more for good measure.

They were married.

YOU'RE HITCHED.

Stella couldn't stop running her thumb over the gold band on her fourth finger.

Not when they returned to camp and no one even seemed to notice their absence. Everyone was busy getting prepared to pull out.

Not when Collin stayed for breakfast at Lily's cook fire, not Alice's. He'd sat close enough beside her that their shoulders kept brushing while they ate. Close enough for her to notice how he favored his injured arm.

And not when they were summoned to speak with Hollis. Rather, *she* was summoned.

It was Owen who came to fetch them. His sharp eyes missed nothing, catching the flash of gold on her finger before his gaze jumped between her and Collin.

She was still shaken, still scanning the campground for signs of Irene as they followed Owen between wagons to where Hollis sat propped against a wagon wheel on the outside of camp. Unless someone was looking for him, no one would know he was out here.

He had a small leather-bound book in one hand and a stub of pencil in the other. He looked peaked and squinted as if the morning sunlight gave him a headache.

If she hadn't known better, she'd say he was as hungover as Coop must be by now. *Head injuries are tricky things,* Maddie had told her. Was that only a day and a half ago? Time seemed to have warped and stretched after Maddie had disappeared from camp.

"Here's Stella." Owen said, drawing Hollis's focus to them. "And Collin. You want me to stay?"

Hollis nodded, then his mouth pulled in a frown, as if the motion had hurt him.

"I've heard about your falsehoods from several sources," Hollis said gravely. "This is your one chance to tell me why you hired on with the wagon train under false pretenses."

The morning breeze felt a little *too* brisk as it blew her skirt against her legs. The sunlight seemed a bit too harsh.

One chance.

She shifted on her feet, words ready to spill out. Their misfortunes. Skate over the wrong choices she'd made.

Collin's hand rested at her lower back, warmth spreading from his touch. Her chest unlocked. She drew a deep breath of spring-scented prairie grass.

Her thinking was wrong. She didn't have one chance.

She had unlimited chances. Because Collin stood by her side. She had his ring on her finger, his promise that he'd stand by her no matter what.

If Hollis kicked her out of the wagon train, she and Collin would figure out a solution together.

She wasn't alone any more.

It was time to stop running.

"Would it be all right if we sit down? Collin is still recovering from his gunshot wound."

Hollis seemed a little relieved not to have to crane his neck to look up at them.

She told him everything that had happened since their arrival off the boat in New York City. How she'd been afraid for her sisters, and the threats. Her decision to partner with Irene, to steal enough money to escape.

Catching Irene with the necklace.

It was a relief to tell the truth. That she hadn't known Irene had stolen it. That she hadn't even known it had existed until it had slipped out of Irene's dress when she'd been ill.

She told him about Irene coming back last night, threatening her with a knife.

Neither she nor Collin knew where Irene had gone. And she didn't want anything to do with a stolen necklace or the woman who'd done it.

"I wanted a safe place for my sisters," she said. "I still want that. A home where they are protected and loved."

Collin glanced at her, and she saw all the love she felt for him reflected back to her.

"That's what we'll give them," he said. "No matter if we get to Oregon this season or next."

"We?" Hollis asked.

Collin's shoulders were straight and his voice confident. "Stella and I married this morning. We met a nice chaplain in the fort who obliged us."

One of Hollis's eyebrows twitched.

It was Owen, leaning on the other end of the wagon and chewing on a blade of grass, who asked. "Leo know about this?"

"He knew my intentions, but I haven't had a chance to speak to him yet today."

Hollis sighed. He tapped his pencil against his book. "I can't condone what you did. Stealing that money."

Her insides squeezed.

"But I understand it."

He did?

"I have sisters. And I can admire that you wanted to protect yours, no matter the cost."

She hadn't had much chance to interact directly with the wagon master. She didn't know his family situation. Even Owen seemed to be wearing a surprised expression.

"We've got a long journey still ahead of us," Hollis said. "These lost days..." He shook his head slightly. Winced. "Your brother is one of the few true leaders on this wagon train," he said to Collin. "And I need you both if we're going to make it across the mountains before the snow sets in."

His gaze swung to Stella. Her heart flew into her throat.

"You and your sisters cause any more trouble, you'll face consequences."

She swallowed the protest she wanted to make. Maddie had been more help than anyone else on this wagon train. Lily hadn't done anything other than dress like a man.

But she was being granted a second chance, and she wasn't going to squander it.

"Understood," she said.

Collin stood and extended his hand to help her up. The movement must've cost him, because she caught his quick grimace.

"Thank you, sir," he said to Hollis.

The man was already squinting down at the book in his lap. Owen had stepped closer to squat next to him, neither one paying any more attention to them.

Stella followed Collin back the direction they'd come. "You need to rest," she chided him. "Did you check your bandage this morning?"

"Not yet, dear."

He shot her a teasing look that made her wrinkle her nose.

He laughed.

"You did it," he said. "You got him to let you stay."

"All I did was tell the truth."

Would it have changed things if she'd approached Hollis in Independence as a woman? She couldn't say.

But things had turned out all right, hadn't they?

Better than all right.

Collin took her hand in his as they walked back toward the wagons.

"Uh oh," he said.

Leo stood waiting for them, arms crossed.

Collin sighed. "I suppose it's my turn to 'fess up."

And then Leo broke into a smile. Behind him, she saw Alice stooped over the fire. Evangeline had Sara on her hip and was talking with Maddie and Lily.

Alice straightened, using her apron to carefully hold a cast iron pan. "You're here!"

"So... are you." Collin's voice held a note of amusement. He held Stella's hand, their fingers threaded together. "What's going on?"

Maddie and Lily turned beaming smiles on them.

"We wanted to celebrate with you," Alice said. She brought the pan toward them. It was filled with what looked like... cornbread?

"Even if you didn't invite us to the wedding," Leo added.

Stella's gaze went to Leo even as Collin focused on the pan.

"Is that . . . cake?" Collin asked.

"Mmhmm." Alice smiled.

Stella was still looking at Leo. "How'd you know?"

"Coop told us." The brothers traded a long glance.

A surreptitious glance around showed that Coop was nowhere to be seen. When they'd left the campsite for the fort, he'd said he was going to sleep. But now he was gone.

There was a tightness to Collin's smile. She squeezed his hand. When he looked at her, the hurt in his eyes softened, though it didn't leave completely. Things might still be difficult with Coop, but they'd get through it together.

"I'll get the plates," said Evangeline, turning to the wagon.

Maddie and Lily came to give Stella hugs.

"You finally listened to our advice," Lily teased her in a whisper.

Alice brought two plates of cake, one in each hand. When Collin let go of Stella to reach for one of them, Alice *tsked* and held the cake out of his reach. "Ladies first," she chided him.

She handed Stella the plate with a slice of fluffy cake she must've baked over the fire. She wore a warm smile. "Welcome to the family."

Welcome.

Stella warmed from the inside out.

She took it all in as Collin was given his cake, as they were given prominent seats in the campsite. She watched the brotherly ribbing from Leo and accepted a hug from Evangeline. Maddie and Lily chatted with Alice as they ate their own pieces of cake.

Welcome to the family.

She'd wanted this feeling of belonging for such a long time. Now she had it, and she couldn't help the tears that smarted in her eyes.

Collin seemed to know. When no one was looking, he snuck her hand back into his.

She hadn't expected him to barrel into her life. Hadn't known she could love someone so much. Or be so loved in return.

God had given her a gift when he'd sent her Collin.

She couldn't wait to finish this journey—together.

TWENTY-THREE

August was sipping a cup of coffee and staring out at the vast prairie unfolded before him when Owen joined him.

His brother had his own cup of coffee in hand, a curl of steam wafting from it.

August would've been content to sit in silence and soak up the beauty around them, but Owen spoke.

"Clarence Turnbull and Elroy Jenkins left the wagon train, along with three other families."

August had known change was coming. It'd been evident in the tensions running throughout the company these past few days. Like the first hint of snow in late fall.

"Two other families from a wagon train that passed through a week ago stopped to repair their wagons. Hollis agreed to let them join."

Owen didn't expect August to answer. He hadn't asked a question. He was only delivering information. August could still remember a time when they'd been small. He'd been maybe... five? And Owen seven. Owen had pestered and pestered August about his quiet nature, how he kept to himself, more content to explore the woods with their hound dog than play tag with Owen and his friends.

As they'd grown up, Owen had stopped bugging August about it.

But he didn't truly feel that Owen accepted him for who he was. Owen still wanted that brother who wanted to sit around the campfire and spin stories, not the one he'd gotten.

"Hollis asked me to find a replacement for Turnbull. We need a new captain."

"No," August said. His voice sounded rusty.

"Hollis needs you. I need you," Owen rushed on when August started to protest. "You're the only one I can trust."

August raised his brows in a disbelieving look. "You've got Leo and Alice now."

They'd made the arduous journey from their California homestead after Pa had died, seeking to make things right with the brother and sister they'd never known about until Pa was on his deathbed.

Owen had formed a tenuous friendship with Leo, though the man hadn't warmed up to August yet. It might've been easier if August had been easier to talk to.

Alice was easy. She seemed to get along with everyone. She had a calming nature about her. She was likable.

"Leo is worried that Evangeline will still be a target, traveling with all that money. And now Collin's gotten himself entangled with the Irish gal."

"So he should hire some hands to ride along."

Leo was a natural-born leader. He made a good captain. Much better than August would.

"He did. Hired on two fellas from the fort. But even with Leo and myself, we need a third captain."

August shook his head. He'd agreed to come along on the wagon train to make sure Leo and Alice arrived in Oregon safely.

He preferred a more solitary existence. In the wagon train, he was surrounded by people day and night.

He didn't need to be put in a position where they'd actively seek him out for help.

Owen glanced around, making no effort to be surreptitious about it.

August did the same out of habit, then snapped himself out of it. What was Owen doing?

His brother lowered his voice. "I was in the room when Hollis got examined by the fort's medic. He said Hollis's head wound didn't look like it'd happened by falling off a horse. Not with how high on the back of his head it was."

August's brows creased. "What caused it, then?"

"Someone hit him over the head."

What?

August's thoughts sharpened. He'd spent three days tracking on his self-imposed mission to find Hollis, though he'd also found Felicity and Abigail's mangled wagon, and two other families besides.

He'd finally found Hollis, unconscious, with a bloody wound on the back of his head. He'd been more worried about getting the wagon master to someone who could help him—namely Maddie—than searching his surroundings.

"He was unconscious for part of a day and night, at least."

"I know," Owen said. "If someone did attack him, they left him for dead."

Wasn't that a comforting thought?

If they'd wanted to kill him, why hadn't they just shot him?

August could make an educated guess. Hollis was skilled with both a rifle and revolver. If you drew on him, you risked getting shot yourself.

So instead, someone'd snuck up on him and struck him over the head?

Coward.

"Why?" August asked.

Owen stared out at the horizon. "I don't know. He can't remember what happened, except for trying to ride ahead of that twister. He was headed to the fort to seek out help."

"But he never made it."

Owen shook his head. "No one at the fort saw him, anyways."

"It coulda been one of the men after Stella and her family."

"Maybe so."

There were too many unknowns. And August didn't like that, either. He wanted to help keep Leo and Alice and their family safe.

Owen sighed. "Hollis is keeping it quiet, but he's in pretty bad shape. The medic says he should stay in bed for a week or two."

August's gaze slid to his brother. "He ain't the kind of man who stays in bed."

"I know," Owen said grimly. "He thinks he's riding out of here, but..." He shook his head.

"Alice got a place in her wagon where he can lay down when his head starts paining him?"

Owen nodded. "He asked me to be his mouthpiece, keep things calm among the company until he gets his strength back."

It was a big responsibility. But one that Owen could handle.

"I need your help," Owen said again. "Your eyes and ears are sharp—"

August was already shaking his head. He dumped the dregs of his coffee in the grass. "And they'll stay that way because they aren't full of silly complaints and petty arguments between people who should know better."

Owen threw up a hand. "I know you're anxious to get back to California and disappear into the woods. Forever alone. I bet you don't even want a wife or kids to keep you company."

August glared at his brother. Why did Owen have to push?

"I do want a wife and kids. Eventually."

Something shifted in the back of Owen's gaze. He looked almost crafty. August wished he hadn't responded to his brother's angry statement.

"How're you going to meet this wife if you're always out trapping?"

August squinted into the distance. "I figure God'll bring her to me when He's good and ready."

Owen made a sound of disbelief. "If you really want to marry, you'd be better off looking on this wagon train for someone who'll have you."

He shook his head.

But Owen wasn't done. "You just said you wanted a wife and kids."

"Eventually."

He had plenty of good years ahead of him.

He disliked the way Owen's eyes glittered. "You've always wanted Pa's homestead for your own."

August's heart banged against his sternum. That was a true statement. He felt an affinity for the land he'd grown up on, the tiny cabin his father had built with his own hands. Ma and Pa were buried there.

"If you find yourself a wife before we reach the Willamette Valley, I'll sign over the deed to you. You'll own Pa's land free and clear."

His thoughts raced. Pa had left the land to Owen, as the oldest son. And August had coveted it since the moment he'd found out.

A shadow moved behind the canvas of the nearest wagon. August glanced over his shoulder, tracking the movement with his eyes.

Felicity was hobbling next to Abigail, leaning heavily on her friend. He must've been really distracted if he hadn't noticed the two women passing by.

"And if you're hunting for a wife, you might as well be captain." Owen's statement brought August out of his distraction.

"I'm not going to be captain," August said. "But I will take your wager. If I get married before Oregon, the homestead is mine."

"UP, LEE!" The little girl's voice carried across the campsite. Felicity watched as Leo Spencer scooped her up into his arms.

Evangeline looked up from the coffee pot where she was adding grounds to the water already inside. "Give me a moment and I'll take her."

"That's all right—"

"I know you're tired. What time did you crawl into bed last night?"

He smiled faintly, looking at the little girl in his arms. "Your—sissy is worried about me, sounds like."

The little girl patted his stubbled cheek. "Lee wurried?"

"Naw."

Evangeline sighed.

Felicity didn't know the man, other than the few days she and Abigail had been staying in his campsite, but she did think he looked a little worn around the edges.

Everyone had been on edge since the tornado. They finally had their wagon master back. They would be packing up and back on the trail again later in the afternoon.

Leo came closer, like he couldn't bear to be too far from his new wife, and sat on a crate near the fire. "We're all she's got left," he said quietly to Evangeline. "Maybe she should start calling us Ma and Pa."

Everyone in the company knew that Evangeline's father had passed away after he'd been shot by a desperate young man, leaving two daughters behind. Evangeline and Sara.

Something passed between Leo and his wife, an unspoken communication. Evangeline glanced down and wiped her hands on her apron as she straightened. "You're probably right."

"Did you hear that, peanut? First time since we got hitched."

Sara giggled as he tickled her side and Evangeline rolled her eyes, but there was something tender and uncertain in her expression.

Leo patted an empty crate next to him. Evangeline sat down, folding her skirts around her legs.

"How are you holding up?" he asked.

She shook her head, and Felicity saw her face crumple.

Leo quickly leaned in and put his arm around her.

Felicity must've made some noise from the corner of camp where she was sitting, because Leo's sharp gaze quickly landed on her.

He nodded, before tipping his head close to Evangeline and murmuring something in her ear.

Sara wiggled free from being sandwiched between them and stood by Leo's knee.

Felicity hadn't meant to intrude on their private family moment.

But she was stuck.

She was still in incredible pain when she stood. Or moved. Or breathed too deeply.

She'd been mostly invisible in her corner of the camp-site. Abigail slept in the Masons' tent. She'd been helping take care of Hollis and also helping with the cooking for more mouths to feed. Alice and Collin and Coop had given up their tent to the two women who were now without a home-on-wheels.

The past two mornings, Abigail had helped Felicity dress in painful slowness, helped her with a simple braid, and then, after an efficient breakfast, Abigail had moved around the company to help whoever needed it.

Felicity felt utterly helpless. She was weaker than a babe, in constant pain.

And every day, she had to watch August and Alice interact.

If you find yourself a wife before we reach the Willamette Valley, I'll sign over the deed to you.

She hadn't meant to eavesdrop on August's conversation with his brother. She'd been slowly shuffling along, leaning heavily on Abigail, as they'd passed his wagon.

The wager sounded like August was going to be looking for a wife.

He probably wouldn't need to look far. Alice lit up whenever he came into camp.

He'd been concerned about her this morning. He'd come in from a watch that had ended just before breakfast and had spent several minutes conversing with Alice in low voices.

After, he'd come to sit next to Felicity with a teasing, "You're still here?"

Where else was she supposed to go? she wondered bitterly now. She couldn't exactly hobble. And she had no wagon where she could hide.

She had been taught from a young age that she was responsible for herself, that she worked to take care of herself—and often her family.

She didn't know how to feel about being reliant on the charity of others.

If the Masons got tired of sheltering and feeding her —*their* food—she and Abigail would be forced to find someone else to help them. Or be stuck out in this wilderness by themselves.

It was a pitiful situation.

Abigail was out there garnering goodwill by helping other families. She could carry her own weight. She was an excellent cook. She could walk.

Felicity couldn't even hobble along, not without excruciating pain. Not fast enough to keep up with the wagon train once it started rolling again.

She hadn't realized she was crying until a tear rolled down her cheek, tickling her neck.

And footsteps sounded nearby. Heading her way.

She reached up to wipe her tear-stained cheeks. She

moved too quickly and pain stabbed her ribs. The gasp she couldn't suppress burned her throat. More hot tears stung her eyes.

"What's all this?"

Of course it would be August, his voice gentle. He sat on the ground next to her as she tried to mop up her face without hurting herself worse.

She held her breath, hoping that would stem the flow of tears.

"I know it's been a difficult couple of days," he said.

There'd been so much enmity in camp. Not everyone was generous like the Spencers and Masons. Men acted aggressively, threatening their neighbors, defending what was theirs as if they were afraid of being stolen from.

It created an unsettled feeling across the entire camp.

But that wasn't the cause of her tears. And she had no voice to tell him so.

"I've got a spot of good news. Maybe it'll cheer you up," he said. "Owen and I borrowed a wagon early this morning and went back to the wreckage of your wagon."

He'd mentioned doing that days ago. She thought he'd forgotten.

"We found most of your clothes, yours and Abigail's. I think they'll be set to rights after a washing. And some of your food barrels were smashed, but not all of them. Coupla books were pretty water-logged. We brought them back, but not sure they'll make it."

The good news buoyed her spirits. She drew in a shuddering breath.

"And I found this. Is it yours?" He extended his hand. In his palm sat her mother's broach. She'd worn it pinned to the inside of her dress every day. In the chaos of her rescue, she hadn't realize that it'd been ripped free. And lost.

New tears filled her eyes at having the precious possession, her only tie to her mother out here, returned.

Thank you. She mouthed the words as she put her palm over his.

For a moment, his fingers folded over hers and warm tingles trickled up her arm. He leaned his shoulder into hers.

He's just being friendly, she reminded herself sternly.

"That's not all. We've found you a wagon. You and Abigail."

What? She and Abigail didn't have the funds to purchase a new wagon. And she hadn't even thought to ask about their animals since the tornado had ripped her world apart.

He seemed to recognize her agitation because he bumped her shoulder again. "Hollis took care of things."

Abigail wouldn't be happy about that. Felicity didn't know the exact nature of the relationship between the two, but Abigail had once told her vaguely that Hollis knew her older brother.

Did it matter if Abigail was angry, if it meant they could continue on the journey?

Felicity was still mulling it over when she glanced up to see Alice walk into camp with her arms full of what looked like wagon canvas.

Felicity leaned away from August so fast that she tweaked her side and spent a breathless moment in pain.

"What're you—?" His confusion was evident in his voice, and the way he glanced from her to Alice and back again.

Could he tell how much she admired him? She was afraid he saw too much. She'd tried to keep her feelings from blooming. She was invisible, an interloper in his camp. She didn't want to become unwelcome.

"You don't think—?" He shook his head. "I guess it might look like that. Our family's still getting used to each other. Alice," he called out. "You wanna tell Felicity here that you're my *sister*?"

Sister.

Oh.

New, hot embarrassment flushed her cheeks. Why was she constantly humiliating herself in front of August?

Alice waved him off, obviously busy. Leo and Evangeline were still in their own world, speaking quietly, with Sara playing at their feet.

Felicity clutched the broach in her hand, kept her face averted.

If you find yourself a wife before we reach the Willamette Valley, I'll sign over the deed to you.

She'd misinterpreted his relationship with Alice. Maybe she'd misunderstood the words shared between the brothers.

He bumped her shoulder once more. "I'm glad we're friends."

Friends.

He stood up, unaware of the turmoil he'd thrust her into. He thought of her only as a friend.

He tipped his hat. "I need a friend like you, Felicity."

He couldn't know how his words cracked her heart open. He had made a bet with his brother to find a wife.

Felicity was right here under his nose. But he didn't see her as wife material. That much was obvious.

He only wanted a friend.

It was only her who'd hoped for more.

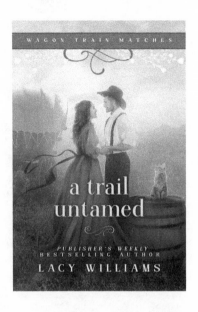

August is a loner and prefers it that way. He only took the marriage wager to gain breathing room from his overbearing older brother. Besides, it's a long way to Oregon. Maybe he'll meet someone who turns his head.

Felicity longs for love and family, someone to choose her above all. After a wagon train accident robs her of her voice and leaves her dependent on the kindness of strangers, she finds herself in August's care. And she can't help falling the spell of a man who shows a deep well of kindness and anticipates her every need.

But August only sees her as a friend. Can a mousy, shy spinster like her win the heart of a man like August?

Read A TRAIL UNTAMED

For my Family.

ACKNOWLEDGMENTS

With heartfelt gratefulness to my friend Benita Jackson for being an early reader of this book. Your insights are a huge help!

Also thank you to my proofreaders Lillian, MaryEllen, Benecia, and Shelley for helping me clean up all the little errors.

Want to connect online? Here's where you can find me:

Get new release alerts

Follow me on Amazon
Follow me on Bookbub
Follow me on Goodreads

Connect on the web

www.lacywilliams.net
lacy@lacywilliams.net

Social media